Red Is a Color

Thomas H Murray

BASTET PUBLISHING

TABLE OF CONTENTS

INTRODUCTORY NOTES

For my readers who are not familiar with how long a meter is try to remember that 1 meter = 1.09 yards. Also, in Europe it is common to use what is called in the US 'military time'. Everything is the same for the first twelve hours of the day until 1 pm, which is 1300. Midnight is 2400.

CHAPTER ONE

The first poison arrow thumped into the middle of Gwendolyn's backpack. Besides the impact, the strange fruity scent of the deadly poison struck her nose. Another arrow grazed the cheek of her indigenous guide.

He yelled, "Run! Let's hide behind that boulder over there!"

They landed behind their rocky shelter. He leaned to the side and fired two shots from his revolver at the odd band of brightly painted, nearly naked bronze-colored men. He missed, but they stopped their pursuit momentarily, finding shelter behind various trees and rocks.

"They're Nitri-Bulachos. What're they doing here? These lands are my tribe's. We need to get out of here. They're god-cursed cannibals!"

"You told me there would be no danger on this trek! Your revolver was only to scare away wild animals, not wild men!"

"I'm sorry. I was wrong. Should have brought a rifle. Look! They caught our pack carriers. That will give us a little time. We need to keep moving."

"But where to?"

"Anywhere but here!"

He sprinted down a secondary trail through scrubland that quickly turned into forest. Gwendolyn had no choice but to follow. As they ran, another barrage of arrows landed nearby.

They dropped behind another large rock. "Let's rest here a few minutes. They don't know how many bullets I have left."

Gwendolyn asked him, "They're all yelling 'ruiva'. What does that mean?"

"It's Portuguese for 'redhead'. If they were from Peru, they would use the Spanish word: 'pelirroja'. As we say in Peru, nothing good ever blows here from Brazil. It's you they want."

"Me? Why me?"

"Maybe they want your red hair. Maybe they want to shrink your head, too."

"My red hair? Shrink my head?"

"How the hell do I know what these savages want? Look, I'll protect you for as long as I can. If I can't, just remember to run north in that direction. You'll find a river there where you can swim to the other side and follow it downriver. There are settlements there. They'll protect you. Do you understand?"

"Yes, I do."

"OK, then let's continue moving towards the river."

He struggled slowly to his feet. "Oh, I'm really getting tired."

They continued running, but after a few minutes, her guide was slowing, panting heavily. He slid down behind a tree and fired his remaining shots at the approaching pursuers. His arm fell to his side. He closed his eyes.

"Come on, Pedro! What are you doing? We have to go!"

"I can't. I'm too sleepy. Must take a nap. You go on ahead. I'll follow in a few minutes." His voice turned into a whisper.

"A nap? Are you crazy? They'll kill us." She tried to pull him up, but the poison had taken hold. His muscles were gradually becoming paralyzed until he could only lie down with his terrified eyes open. Even his mouth no longer had the power to form words.

She sprinted down the same path. The tribals briefly paused when they found the paralyzed guide. Their greed urged them on to capture the young white woman rapidly disappearing into the trees with her long red hair flowing behind her.

Gwendolyn ran as fast as her burning lungs and legs allowed. She cursed, "Damn you, Giles! What another fine mess you put me in! I agreed to Machu Picchu, but not this!"

Trying to lose her pursuers, she veered off the path, cutting through the forest. But these were highly skilled hunters chasing her. Her every step crushed a plant or broke a stick. She might as well have had a fire alarm ringing in her backpack.

As long as there were trees between them, they had no clear shot. Suddenly she entered a clearing of brush. She continued forward until she halted at the edge of a cliff. She peered over the precipice at the sheer drop of fifty meters to the river rapids below.

They stopped, forming a semi-circle around her, bows held up, not fifteen meters away. Steadily, they closed the distance. There was no way they could miss her now.

Sweat pouring down her face, Gwendolyn reacted in pure survival instinct. Without thinking, she ran towards them, shrieking as if possessed by unclean spirits, causing them to step back in confusion. What was this crazy branca doing?

She pivoted around and sprinted toward the cliff edge. Her pursuers gasped as she leapt off and away from the cliff as far as she could. Screaming all the way, she plunged into the cold, turbulent river. She found the surface and breathed deeply though with little relief, having swapped poison arrows for probable drowning.

The rushing water carried her along, too fast to reach the riverbanks. The force of the current banged her against submerged rocks. Bruised and bleeding, she struggled to hold her head above the water. Panic gripped her heart as she realized the river disappeared ahead.

A waterfall!

Over the edge, she fell, and everything went black.

*****

Gwendolyn slowly opened her eyes. Whiteness nearly blinded her. A white room, white people, and heavenly white sunlight surrounded her.

She cried out weakly, "I did it! I made it to heaven!"

She rolled over and fell back to sleep. Her cry caused a flurry of activity as the white-robed nurses of a holy order crowded around her, discussing what to do. A doctor strode into the room, immediately taking charge.

He murmured into her ear, "Gwendolyn. Gwendolyn. It's time to wake up. Breakfast is waiting. Would you like a cup of coffee?"

His words gradually seeped into her consciousness. The words 'breakfast' and 'coffee' touched a chord. Her groaning stomach prompted her eyes to open.

She whispered, "Yes, dear angel, I would like that. Are you Gabriel?"

"No. More like Azazel, but you can call me Dave."

"Azazel? Where am I?" She tried to sit up but fell back onto her pillow.

"You are at the medical clinic in Santa Maria. You nearly drowned. A boat of the local environmental protection office was searching for illegal timber thieves when they saw you fall over the cascade. They brought you here three days ago. Only now you are conscious."

"I only remember cannibals chasing me. I managed to escape only by jumping off a cliff into the river."

"Hold on. Did you say 'cannibals'? What gives you that idea?"

"Yes. They were a band of dark red men, I mean really red, who painted themselves in various geometric designs. They wore what looked like grass skirts and nothing else. They attacked us with poisoned arrows. One hit my guide and killed him. All it did was graze his cheek. It was terrible!"

"Very strange. Did your guide give them a name?"

"He called them Nitri-Bulachos. He said they were cannibals and headhunters. That they wanted my red hair."

"How do you know it was your red hair they were after? This story is getting stranger by the moment."

"They kept shouting 'ruiva', which my guide told me is Portuguese for 'redhead'."

"OK, I have to stop you there. The Nitri-Bulachos are neither headhunters nor cannibals. That's an old legend the neighboring peoples use to malign each other. Most of them have names like Maria and Tiago. They go to church on Sunday and wear normal clothes. They don't live too far from here.

We could visit them if you'd like. The fact that they spoke Portuguese means they went to a Brazilian public school where they learned it. I doubt there's anyone in this region who would hunt with anything other than a hunting rifle."

"But why then were they dressed the way they were, hunting us with poison arrows, and yelling 'ruiva'?"

"You know what it sounds like to me? They were probably a group of adolescent boys high on something, maybe coca leaves, out to scare a tourist, and it got out of hand."

Regaining her strength, she sat up successfully this time. "It got out of hand? It got out of hand?? They killed our two supply carriers and my guide. They were grown men, not teenagers. The look in their eyes was more insane than high. If I hadn't jumped off that cliff, they would've killed me. I have no doubt of that."

"OK, Gwendolyn, we'll just have to leave it at that. Let's change the subject."

"Wait a minute! How do you know my name?"

"You thought I was the angel Gabriel when you first woke up. You seem familiar with angels, and they definitely are familiar with you, because you have one, a guardian angel named Giles. God only knows how he found me, but he did."

"Giles? Oh, no! I forgot to call and check in with him. Where's my phone?"

"Your phone is thoroughly drenched. You could use mine, but on my salary, I have no idea what that call would cost me."

"Is there a bank or an ATM in this town? I could use my credit card to withdraw money and pay you in advance. Do you think USD100 would cover it? USD200?"

"No, no, it wouldn't cost that much for a quick call. Tell you what. After you return to wherever you are from, make a generous donation to the Upper Amazon Conservancy. I am a medical advisor for them, spending a lot of my time treating the indigenous peoples."

"I detect a mid-Western US accent. How did you get here?"

"I came as a fervent Mormon missionary, full of faith and the desire to seek martyrdom. But after living with these people for a while, I converted to open-minded humanism. Once UAC offered me work, actual meaningful work, I decided to stay. Hey, my phone is ringing… Yes. Yes, she is indeed right here. Do you want to talk to her? It's for you." He handed her his phone.

"Giles! I am so angry with you! When I see you next, I'm going to wring your neck. But first get me out of here! I was almost eaten by cannibals! Where did you say? Lisboa, Portugal? Fine, just arrange for me to get there. Dave. Here, he wants to talk to you…"

CHAPTER TWO

Lisboa, the second oldest capital city of Europe, spread out below Gwendolyn's window as her flight approached Humberto Delgado Airport. She sighed loudly in great relief as she stepped off the plane. It seemed like hundreds of years ago she was recovering from nearly dying in a remote Peruvian village on the banks of a tributary of the Amazon. She decided that she would never go trekking remotely ever again.

She stepped through the sliding doors into the crowded arrival hall. There was Giles holding a large colorful sign above his head with the words: "Welcome, dearie pip! Please don't be angry!" She had been determined to be angry with him, but she just did not have it in her. It was not his fault that a team of head-hunting cannibals far from home tried to hunt her for her red hair and tender meat.

Rushing through the crowd to where he was standing, she hesitated for a moment, trying to feign anger, but quickly dropped her luggage and hugged him tightly. "Damn you, Giles! I should be furious with you, but I can't help myself. Thanks for everything. Now what?"

"Now we get you to the Four Seasons to freshen up before dinner. We have so much to talk about!"

After showering and changing her clothes, she still had time before meeting Giles. She strolled through the nearby Parque Eduardo VII up to the terrace at the higher northern end. There with an espresso she savored the incredible view of the city below her, rolling down to the edge of the Tejo River. She decided that after her adventures in the wilds, it would be best to stick close to cities in her future. The only dangers she faced in Lisboa would be handsome cinnamon-colored men with a five-day stubble flirting with her. That was a danger she would very willingly face any day.

Gwendolyn met Giles in the lobby at the appointed hour. He wore a disguise that made him look like Fernando Pessoa or another Portuguese poet of the 1920s. They took a taxi to Paço de Arcos, where the Tejo River meets the Atlantic Ocean.

"I see, Giles, you're still in form with your disguises. Why didn't you wear one at the airport in the middle of thousands of people?"

He replied, "Who says I wasn't wearing a disguise then? I might really be a young woman in her twenties like you. On to more serious things. Aside from telling me what exactly happened in Peru, if you want, I would like to relate to you our next project, if you're up for it. We'll dine at an excellent traditional Portuguese restaurant where I know the owners. They'll leave us alone. Apparently, we are related in an obscure distant way. It's also small enough that I can reserve the whole place just for us. No need to have eavesdroppers."

The taxi stopped in front of a simple restaurant that was closed. Just one car could fit on the cobblestone lane, with doors able to open on only one side. No space separated the doors of the traditional shops and narrow row houses from the street. Clearly, people built them during the era of horses.

After the taxi left, Gwendolyn looked for an open restaurant. "OK, Giles, where is it? Everything is closed here."

"My dear girl, it's right here." Giles rapped hard on the window. At once, lights lit up the dark interior. A moment later, the door opened. A kind faced middle-aged gentleman stepped out and grabbed Giles' hand. "Welcome, welcome, my dear cousin. Please do come in!"

Giles motioned for Gwendolyn to enter first. There the owner's wife, matronly partner of the establishment, greeted her with a hug and two kisses on her cheeks. She managed the kitchen, and he serviced the patrons. Many younger family members helped in various ways. It was a true family venture run by the descendants of the patriarch who founded it in 1956.

"Please, come over here. This is your table. We and the entire restaurant are at your disposal. Our specialty is the cuisine of Alentejo." He handed them two menus. Giles ordered Bacalhau à Brás. Gwendolyn ordered grilled porco preto (black pork), made from the meat of a free-ranging pig, which eats mainly acorns and grass. He chose a white wine from the Vidigueira winery in south central Alentejo and a bottle of Flor de Sal, a red wine from further east of Alentejo, very close to the Spanish border.

The typical entrees of Portugal - olives, several types of cheese, and fresh bread - covered the table. The walls held mounted antique ceramic dishes of different sizes, designs, and colors. Cobalt glass wine bottles hung from the ceiling containing electric lights inside, illuminating the restaurant with a bluish-tinged light. Another wall displayed a dozen antique hunting rifles that appeared too dangerous to use. An enormous stone fireplace with a huge brass cooking pot hanging by wrought iron chains filled a different wall. The floors were long wooden planks. Similar wooden rafters intersected the ceiling.

While they were waiting for the food, the elderly senhor arrived to pour the wine. First, he offered Giles to taste them both. Giles did and smiled with approval. He then filled Gwendolyn's two glasses followed by Giles' glasses, each glass with either the white or red. After performing that ritual, he placed the bottle of white in a bucket of ice and water that was sitting on a small stand within arm's reach of Giles. He tied a white cloth around the neck of the bottle of red and placed it on the table.

Gwendolyn nodded in approval after she tasted both wines. She pointed to the bottle of red as her preferred choice to pair with her meal. Giles took this as a signal to begin. "OK. I'll start. The winery of the white wine is close to a town in Alentejo called Cuba, about two hours south of here by car. There you will find statues of Christopher Columbus in the town plazas and main thoroughfares named after him. The tourist office has a museum in a side room, which explains that Columbus was born there and not in Genoa, where the rest of the world thinks.

"Their principal argument is that Columbus named the island Cuba, which he discovered on his first voyage in 1492 after his Portuguese birthplace. I mean, why not? OK, now that I have opened the subject of the New World for you, it's your turn to share an interesting story that recently happened in that hemisphere."

Gwendolyn drank deeply from her wine glass and related to him both her pleasant and harrowing experiences in Peru. When she finished, Giles only shrugged and said, "Poisoned arrows, did you say? I wonder why they didn't use poisoned blow darts. Maybe arrows have a greater range than darts?"

He paused and noticed the exasperation rising in her face. He hastened to add with all his charm, "In the end, Uncle Giles came to the rescue and now you're back in civilization again."

She laughed when he said 'Uncle'. Dropping any residue of anger, she continued. "Fine, dear 'Uncle', I suppose I should thank you for the generous life experiences you've given me. You'll probably tell me next how all experiences, good and bad, build character. Please don't. So what's our next escapade? I thought we owed Dimitri in Moscow a reward for his gallantry to me?"

"Ah, yes, Dimitri. We'll do that another time. Russia is currently a pariah state for obvious reasons. An interesting opportunity has recently presented itself in the past few weeks right here. Let me explain."

Giles laid out their new project. "An eccentric anglophile Portuguese man in his mid to late seventies lives in Estoril about a twenty-minute drive west from here. Hanging over his fireplace is a life-sized painting of a standing nude woman with nymphs. Luisa, his housekeeper and mistress, lives with him.

"Interestingly, he started his early adult years thinking he was gay. Then, when he reached his fifties, he realized he was in truth heterosexual, left his husband/wife, and returned to his home in Portugal for a woman. It's unusual to lose one to the other team. He made up the lost decades of his repressed sexuality in a surprisingly short time. His name is Rui Manuel de Pinheiro Silveira. Pronounced as I just did. Huwee and not like Sister Ray. Do you know who she is?"

"Sister Ray? Of course, I know her. You're not the only one who's familiar with your country's Joy Division. Besides, I studied a semester in Iberian Art History. I know how to pronounce the names. Please, stay on task."

"Joy Division? I was thinking of your country's Velvet Underground, the original creators of the odd sister. OK, back on task. Rui has a keen eye for attractive young women, even if it's only for their aesthetic beauty. He fancies himself as an artist. He is also very fond of dogs. Every morning, he walks his five Dalmatians on a set route. You can enter his odd world by painting a seascape on his way which passes the ocean every day until he takes notice. If you're willing to save time, you could paint wearing a bikini."

"Oh, yeah right. What am I supposed to do, sleep with the old man? Not happening."

"If you were German, you would paint topless, just for the pure joy of it."

"Giles, you're not helping your cause."

"Look, you can do whatever you want. You're an expert at catching whales with a fishing line."

"Get on with it! What about the painting?"

He continued. "According to our client, Rui's painting has a strange cult following with mysterious beliefs. They occasionally have rituals dancing in front of it, or whatever middle-aged men with very fertile imaginations do when they've had too much to drink. Our client has participated in many of them. I can't really tell you any more about it. He was quite vague on that point.

"Our client, himself a devoted follower of the goddess, is willing to pay an astonishing sum for the miraculous transfer of ownership. The painting is a close copy of Botticelli's Birth of Venus by a student of his whose name escapes history or perhaps, as our client strongly believes, even by the great master himself. I'm sure Rui could tell you more. If the Uffizi Museum in Florence knows anything about it, they're not telling. I've asked."

Giles paused for her reaction. She did not disappoint him.

"Did you say Botticelli's Birth of Venus?" She nearly sputtered out her wine.

"Yes, you heard correctly. Naturally, I will pay twice your normal fee, considering how generous the new owner to-be is. Are you interested?"

"You nearly lost me with your painting topless comment. But I consider Botticelli a worthy professional challenge. What else can you tell me?"

"Remember, it might not be by Botticelli. It doesn't matter. Whatever it is. Just reproduce it exactly. The major difference between the paintings is that Rui's Venus is not covering her private parts with her hand or hair.

"She is also, how should I put it, more voluptuous and more wanton. She's no pure, demure virgin being born immaculately by rising from the sea on a seashell. Perhaps Rui's Venus was an unreformed mermaid who had gone through further modification by changing her fish body for legs. The future owner showed me a photo."

"Giles, I will copy in every detail the painting that is hanging above Rui's fireplace. If she has gills, I'll reproduce that, too."

"Great. Now let's think of the reason you're in Portugal."

"Let's see. I could be a globetrotting professional artist looking for a place to settle down. I thought I would give Portugal a try."

"Wonderful, and it's even true. That makes it more believable."

"Anything else I should know?"

"About the only other thing I can tell you is the painting is lifelike and large: two meters by one and a half."

"I'll need at least two or three months to do it. I hope I won't overstay my welcome with Rui. That will be the biggest challenge."

"He owns several cork forests and olive groves. He often visits them by flying his single-engine plane there with Luisa. She now serves as his caregiver, though there was a time when she was much more. You could have the place mostly to yourself. In any case, the future caregiver of the painting has not given us a deadline.

"Here's another angle. He studied naval architecture at the University of Strathclyde in Glasgow. Following that, he gained experience working in several of the UK's leading yacht design and construction companies. He had a nasty experience over patents with ruthless and dishonest partners. One was even his own brother. After a period of twenty-some years, he returned to Portugal. Did I mention he's an ardent anglophile?"

"Yes, Giles. Keep it together."

"I'd say if you spoke with an English accent, you'd have him eating out of your hand. Speak like I do. Come now. Try it."

"There isn't enough money in the world to make me speak the way you do or in any other way than how I already speak. I'm not a standup comedian. Besides, I'd have to invent a whole upper class fake life to support it."

"Very well. As you wish. I was merely suggesting a way to make it easier for you."

"Are you doubting my ability to manipulate older men?"

"Not with your track record."

"Fine. How do I start?"

"You just arrived from Peru. I want you to take a week or more and learn the lay of the land. Play tourist. When you're ready, let me know and we'll get started."

CHAPTER THREE

Gwendolyn took Giles' advice and wandered the streets of the central neighborhoods of Lisboa for a few days to recover from her jetlag. On the morning of her fourth day, she took the light rail out to Estoril to study the lay of the land, as Giles had put it. She found the address he gave her and sauntered past Rui's aged house. Someone had carefully closed all the curtains, hiding the interior.

The following morning, she arrived just as the sun was rising, discreetly standing within sight of the front gate. Knowing that dogs need to be walked early in the morning, she knew she would not have to wait long. Within twenty minutes, Rui did not disappoint her. She looked up from her e-book to the sound of five dogs barking, excitedly struggling at their leashes.

She tailed him for the entire route, deciding where the best place would be for Rui to notice her. The Dalmatians knew where to go, pulling him first up the hill to where the old mansions merged into wooded scrubland. Then down to the ocean's edge by the pedestrian only Paredão. There, she found the most conspicuous spot to set up her easel. It had a wonderful view of rocks, yachts, and waves. She also noted he passed by there around 0820 with the sun in full ascent.

Gwendolyn changed hotels to be much closer to where she would lay her snare. She checked into the Palacio Hotel across from the Estoril Casino, made famous by Ian Fleming's first novel, Casino Royale, and where he served as a British spy during the Second World War. It was only a five-minute walk to where she would pose as an innocent lamb, tempting a passing wolf.

She started the intricate dance by placing her easel at an angle to view both the sea and anyone passing by yet placing it in such a way that a passerby could see her painting. Instead of a bikini, she substituted shorts and a halter top. She had barely begun painting the base in broad strokes when he strode by with his dogs, accompanied by another man of the same age. Giles did not tell her anything about who he might be.

He stopped, turned his attention to Gwendolyn, and spat. "Do you see that, Rui? A redhead! The color only a goddess should have. These imposters should all just die!"

Rui only noticed a young woman starting to paint on a fresh canvas. He shook his head and answered, "Now, George, control yourself. She's an artist. Perhaps she only dyed her hair red. Even if she didn't, maybe she's Irish. There are countries full of natural redheads. I've told you so many times the color of a woman's hair is no reason to hate her. Besides, I know for a fact you have no problem with red-headed men. What is it with you? You really should get professional help. Let's continue our discussion." He pulled his spiteful friend away.

Gwendolyn froze with her brush barely touching the canvas. A chill went up her spine and her legs became weak. She had to sit on the nearby bench. Despite repeating the hateful words in her mind several times, she could make no sense of what she just heard. She needed a moment to calm her racing heart.

She became calmer by reminding herself that, unlike his friend, Rui's voice was filled with gentle kindness. She needed to concentrate on him anyway. Hoping she would never meet the evil-minded other one again, she rose and continued painting until she created a more concrete seascape. She decided to paint in the manner of Botticelli as a subliminal attraction.

With each passing day, Rui walked past slower, and more importantly, closer. But he still was not biting, and her painting neared   its logical end. Then it hit her. She needed an obvious bait to force him to interact. She painted a yacht that happened to lay at anchor a short distance away gently rising and falling with the gentle waves. But she purposely portrayed it shorter than it truly was.

The bait worked. The next morning, Rui stopped. "Young woman, I've noticed you painting our beautiful seaside with the style of Botticelli. It is or was wonderful until you painted the yacht. May I suggest you make it longer as it really is? That is a Rustler 44, built in Falmouth, Cornwall. Based on your proportions, it would resemble a Rustler 36, which does not exist. Furthermore, the yacht you created I would not trust it to sail out of sight of land. It would blow over with the first gust of strong wind.

"It should be a bit more than a quarter longer. You also painted a rudder, while there clearly isn't one visible. It uses a skeg-hung rudder hidden below the keel. Speaking of the keel, I designed that particular one to be a long cord keel. That means it can sail in shallower waters, though it does become less stable in rough seas. But, otherwise, I love it! My name is Rui, by the way."

"Would the yacht look better like this?" Gwendolyn made the suggested changes, pleased that her simple ruse was so successful. He nodded. She continued, "So, you're a yacht designer?"

"Was. I was a naval architect. But it's a bitter story, one that I'd rather not ruin such a wonderful day."

"Sounds like you're Scottish. Wait. Don't tell me. Let me guess. Um… definitely not Edinburg. Glasgow. You're from Glasgow. Did I guess right?"

He smiled, obviously pleased by her feigned mistake. "No. I'm Portuguese actually. I went to the University of Strathclyde in the center of Glasgow. Maybe that's where I picked up the local accent. But enough about me. Let's talk about you. What fair wind blew you to our sun-kissed shores?"

"Well, I recently received my MFA from Yale and decided to travel the world to look for a place that would inspire me to launch my art career. I only arrived nearly a week ago. Already I feel inspired."

"Where are you staying now?"

"I'm staying at the Palacio Hotel."

"Excellent choice. Have you had breakfast yet?"

"About an hour ago, I had an espresso and a croissant. Painting makes me hungry. I could take a break about now. Would you like a cup of coffee in the Palacio's garden?"

"I usually have breakfast after I walk my dogs. My housekeeper prepares a hardy British breakfast, the best breakfast there is. It's a brunch really. I would be honored if you joined us. I'm a bit of an artist myself. I'd greatly appreciate an expert's critique and advice on my paintings. Please say 'yes'."

"Hm, a strange man I only now met is asking me into his home. I suppose this is when I should play coy and politely refuse."

"Oh, you have nothing to worry about on my account. I am, alas, completely harmless."

"Now Rui, I don't believe you're completely harmless." She gave him a smile that would surely waken the sap in an ancient oak. "Oh, why not? We artists are supposed to be free spirits, right? Besides, I'm curious what kind of house would be the home of these magnificent animals. Let me just pack up my painting."

"Yes, indeed we are free spirits. The Palacio is on the way. We'll pass right by it. You can drop off your things there."

"Lead on, Rui."

Back in her room, she dropped her things and changed into a more conservative skirt and blouse with a silk scarf worn in the European style. Gwendolyn stared out her window overlooking the hotel garden and the spacious park leading up to the casino on her right. She enjoyed the grand fountain shooting jets of water high above in the grassy expanse rolling down from the casino towards the beach below. She smiled at how easy it was to catch a whale in such a short time with a simple fishing line, as Giles put it. She turned and headed down to rejoin Rui.

They continued up the hill past the Estoril Congress, the meeting hall for major international conferences. They passed the entrance to the casino, turned right, eventually reaching a steep cobble-stoned street. He stopped in front of his home, extended his arm with a flourish.

"Here we are. My humble abode."

The three-story stone edifice had subtle touches of Art Nouveau, such as nude nymphs and nature motifs. It fit perfectly in with the other houses of Estoril, many of which were mansions of the lesser noblemen who wanted to be near their King as he developed sports and oceanography in nearby Cascais 150 years before. The path to the front door was flanked by six statues of nude maidens, arms slightly outstretched to their sides and heads bent demurely, welcoming their master home.

Gwendolyn was pleased that the coy young women were Art Nouveau and not the ponderously draped Gothic hags normally found in cemeteries. If they were, she would have spun around and abandoned the project right then and there. Rui closed the stout iron gate behind them and released the dogs to run freely around the garden. He opened the heavy wooden front door, dark with age, and beckoned for her to enter.

He led her to a glassed-in sunroom reaching into the southern side of the garden. A table heavily laden with a proper British brunch fit for at least a nobleman welcomed them. Someone appeared behind them, visibly surprised by Gwendolyn's presence. Rui hurriedly introduced Gwendolyn to Luisa, a woman in her fifties who was clinging to the beauty of her disappearing youth. He took the tact that the professional advice of an accomplished artist would be very helpful to his painting.

Luisa, nonetheless, regarded her with suspicion, indicating that she certainly was much more than a housekeeper. She held out her hand, which Gwendolyn accepted with a gentle squeeze. Luisa silently shrugged and turned to bring another place setting for their new guest.

The sun flooded the glassed-in space, warming it nicely. They took their places, plates were filled, and coffee was poured. Gwendolyn regaled them with her misadventures in Peru, deciding to drop that country from her list of possible homes. She already had Rui's attention. Now she had to win over Luisa.

She kept the conversation at the level of artistic professional with occasional anecdotes thrown in. Rui, for his part, stayed on script. He clearly was the master of his home, but still understood that keeping Luisa content was in his best interest. As for Gwendolyn, she was eager to see the special painting. The pleasant preliminaries had to be done. After two and a half hours, Rui suggested he show her his house and the art that occupied such a significant part of it. It was soon clear that Rui's taste ran the short distance between Art Nouveau and the Pre-Raphaelites.

They started on the top floor and worked their way down. First, he showed her a spacious studio apartment that took up the entire floor with a view of the ocean. Rui hinted it would be a perfect spot for a resident artist to stay while she searched for her own place in Portugal. The next floor below had four bedrooms with a long Turkish carpet running the length of the hall.

Paintings of young long-haired nude nature nymphs with crowns of flowers similar to the women one might have found at a 1960s hippy commune dominated the walls. Interspersed between them were wooden stands in the shapes of tree roots and branches, holding sculptures of things like sphinxes, harpies, sirens, and other dangerous womanly characters of mythology. The walls were covered in complex hand-painted geometric floral patterns with many large water birds added for good measure. There were many stained-glass windows with black wrought iron framing each glass pane.

At last, they reached the ground floor, where the object of her professional interest waited. Yet Rui showed her every other room first, as if tantalizing her by waiting until the end to show the pièce de résistance. By the time they entered the dining room, she had seen nearly every example of the few art genres of his narrow taste in interior decoration.

Finally, they reached the living room with its enormous stone fireplace. Above it was Venus, rising from the watery depths on her scallop shell in all her womanly glory. Despite her 500 years, she looked almost modern. The painting's style fit exactly within Rui's artistic palate. It made sense since Botticelli's was one of the paramount examples of what Renaissance art was before Raphael.

In Botticelli's most famous version, Venus tries to be modest while not wearing a stitch of clothing. She appears innocent with a pensive smile, her thoughts lying elsewhere. Not so Rui's Venus. She was undeniably the Goddess of Physical Love, unveiled as she was meant to be. This Aphrodite, originally of ancient Greece, the Venus of the Romans, revealed herself without modesty. Clearly, she did not know what the word meant. Her face gazed directly at the viewer, revealing a lust for life with all its pleasures. Gwendolyn had to admit that she preferred this version to the one in the Uffizi Museum. She stood in awe.

Rui broke the spell by touching her arm, suggesting that they sit in the two easy chairs facing the fireplace with the masterpiece above it. She slowly lowered herself to the chair without taking her eyes off the highly intriguing masterpiece.

"I see you appreciate it. Allow me to tell you what I know about it."

CHAPTER FOUR

"Have you seen Botticelli's original at the Uffizi Museum in Florence?"

"Indeed, I have. Spending a semester in Florence was required for my MFA degree. But this is different in many details."

"Then I won't repeat what you already know about the wonderful Renaissance painter Botticelli. I'll just summarize what little we understand of this painting before us. To start, it has been in my family for at least two hundred years. We have no idea how we acquired it. Experts from the Uffizi Museum itself have verified that it indeed came from the great master's studio.

"All the evidence indicates that the excellent master himself painted it. Filippino Lippi was the only student of Botticelli's few who had anywhere close to the talent to pull this off. But his style is different and, in any case, had already left his mentor's employ on his own successful career long before Botticelli painted it in 1485.

"Though it is possible that another nameless assistant painted it based on a drawing Botticelli had done, I doubt it. After much research, my conclusion is that the great man painted it himself for his own use with his own taste and not that of the patron commissioning it. As you know, it was not until modern times that artists and composers created any work not commissioned by a rich patron. And yet they did for their own enjoyment, as rare as it was.

"The Uffizi offered to buy it for thirty-two million Euros. I could never part with it and not only because it has been in the family for hundreds of years. No, not even because it was painted by the great man himself and that is something to be proud of. It's simply because this is not an object for me. This woman rising from the sea on her shell is my mistress, my muse, my goddess. I worship her..." His voice trailed off into silence.

Gwendolyn did not dare disturb his silence. She felt a pang of regret that she took on the project of exchanging it for her copy. This painting clearly was not yet another possession by a rich man to show off to his friends during a cocktail party. He was emotionally, even spiritually, attached to it.

Rui continued, "Sorry about that. Sometimes my feelings for her so fill my heart, they overpower me. Let's continue. Rather than I tell you, why don't you tell me what you notice is different between the two?"

Gwendolyn cleared her throat and started, "Let's start by summing up what we are seeing. Aphrodite to the Greeks, or Venus to the Romans and Botticelli, was born by rising from the sea on a shell fully grown. Zephyr, the gentle west wind, and harbinger of Spring, locked in an embrace with his mate, Chloris, a nymph of Spring and flowers, are gently blowing Venus towards land. There Flora will soon meet her on the shore, the Roman equivalent of Chloris, holding out a cloak to clothe the naked goddess, soon to be within reach. Flora is the root of flower and of Florence, where Botticelli was born and died. I won't comment on the oddity that Chloris and Flora are the same nymph. Good for Zephyr.

"Flowers play a large role here. The divine couple are blowing them towards Venus. They form the floral patterns on both the robe offered to her by Flora and Flora's own dress. Flora is standing under a grove of orange trees. These all represent Spring, the year's most fertile season.

"I must also add that though Venus was born from the sea, and we see her here being blown to her homeland of Cypress, on the shores are bulrushes and cattails; both are freshwater plants. They're never seen on salty shores. But if we can accept that a fully grown woman can rise from the depths on a scallop shell, we can accept that anomaly, too.

"OK, now let's move on to the differences from the original. The obvious one is Venus herself. She is facing us directly, holding our eyes with hers. She has lowered her right arm below her breasts with no attempt to cover them. Botticelli also modified them from 'B' cups to 'C'. As for the other important part of her feminine anatomy, her hair is no longer covering it. Instead, her hand is, or rather, two fingers are concealing that part. Or maybe 'concealing' is not what she is doing. She is probably inciting us to become her devotees."

Rui blurted, "I never noticed it that way before. Thank you for that insight, an insight only a woman would have. Nonetheless, I am one of her strongest devotees. Please, do go on."

"All the women had red hair in the original, a hair color not normally associated with Italians. They still do here, but it is a darker shade of red, closer to an Irish-Setter red. Kind of like mine, come to think of it. Her long hair still follows the curve from her neck, shoulder, and arm to her leg. Here, too, Chloris now has 'C' cups. The women are beautiful in every loving detail with full womanly bodies, but not at all what I would call Rubenesque. His taste in women is quite modern.

"So, if this is Botticelli's preferred personal version, as opposed to the one in the Uffizi, meant for the wall of a Medici villa, it tells us a lot about the man. He clearly admires the physical charms we women have, especially being slender with well-rounded breasts. He likes them to be very forward without an ounce of coy shyness, but with sweet and beautiful faces.

"There are those who use the fact he never married to say he was gay. That simply isn't true. There were rumors at the time that he had relations with several of his models, including this one, reputed to be a Medici mistress. That would follow in the classical tradition of Pliny's story. Alexander the Great commissioned the artist Apelles to paint a work of the same subject. He gave the artist one of his mistresses to serve as the model for Aphrodite. Apelles fell in love with her, and Alexander magnanimously gave her to him as a gift. This also proves that Alexander was not gay, either. Perhaps bi, but not gay as we define such things today.

"Do you agree with anything I've said? If not, I'd love to hear your version."

Rui sat speechless, staring at the painting. Finally, he broke the silence. "By the gods, Gwendolyn! Where have you been all this time? You have explained this rather mysterious family heirloom perfectly. I cannot add or subtract from it. You'd be an excellent art history professor."

"Nah, I prefer being an artist. At least I'm paid properly for my time. Something I could consider for retirement. Anyway, I'm glad you liked my little lecture."

They continued to discuss Botticelli's Birth of Venus, Botticelli's other paintings, even Botticelli himself. Eventually, their conversation drifted to art in general. The shadows on the floor were becoming longer. Gwendolyn needed a break from the somewhat tiring part conversation and part art lecture. She stifled a yawn.

Rui noticed and quickly suggested they visit his still sunny studio, surrounded by his lovely garden. He wanted her opinion of his paintings. She happily agreed, pleased at how close to success she was with Rui, a man she had just met six hours before.

As soon as Rui opened the door, the aroma of turpentine and oil paint rushed to greet them. It was the smell of painters' studios everywhere and always compelled Gwendolyn to want to reach immediately for a brush and put paint to canvas. From the studio, an artist's hand could capture the perfect light of the afternoon sun on the garden's flowers and statues.

The well-lit studio was the size of a small apartment, complete with a daybed and bathroom. Rui disappeared into a side room where he stored his hundreds of paintings, if they were not hanging on a friend's or his own walls. He noisily shuffled things around. Finally, he reappeared with a dozen paintings, which he arranged on easels for her to critique.

"I painted all of these within the past year. They represent a phase I've been in for some years now. What do you think? Don't hold back."

Gwendolyn most certainly had to hold back. She had to win Rui's confidence and gain his invitation to stay. She stopped herself as she was about to make a long exhale and say something that might be unpleasant or perhaps offensive to Rui.

An unpolished but talented amateur created them. They were of a style between Botticelli and the Neo-Raphaelites. The subjects were so similar, namely nudes in various poses and surroundings. Some paintings had nude men, but all had nude women. Or more accurately, they all were of the same woman.

The woman had the same body and expression as the one hanging above his fireplace. The paintings had one or two men, never more. They, both or singularly, were always in an amorous embrace with her and clearly aroused. The paintings were only a step away from being pornographic.

At least one of the men always had the face of Rui. 'Fair enough', thought Gwendolyn. But the face of the other man shocked her. It certainly was Luisa's face. That realization silenced her for some moments as she pondered all the possible meanings of it. She remembered Giles telling her of Rui's pre-hetero past and decided to leave it at that. Rui was impatiently staring at her, waiting for her assessment.

"Well? Are they that bad that they leave you speechless?"

"No, no, Rui." She quickly snapped back into her role, giving his arm a light reassuring squeeze. "They are very intriguing. Botticelli and the wonderful painting above your fireplace clearly inspired you. But you have modernized them with the art nouveau style of the Pre-Raphaelites and their fascination with redhead women. It makes sense since the Pre-Raphaelites took Botticelli's century as their inspiration, the so-called Quattrocento movement."

Rui nodded. "Yes, you are exactly correct. What a good eye you have. I think Leonardo da Vinci, Raphael, and Michelangelo are overrated. But that is a subject for another time. Please go on."

"Ah, OK. Of course, the Birth of Venus does not have much detailed nature in it, but Botticelli's Primavera certainly does. So, back to your paintings. The colors are vivid with no shortage of details. Many details and perspectives are almost modern in their blurring between strict reality and artistic expression. Maybe there is some Cezanne influence here?

"And that one there clearly had Manet's Olympia in mind. But you made it yours by changing the African woman servant behind her to a young, virile Davidesque man servant, eager to please her. Oh, sorry. You don't like Michelangelo. Fine, we can pick any other admirer of the physical body, instead, whether man or woman.

"The subject matter is interesting in your choice of poses. Clearly, the fertility forces of Mother Nature are very evident. There are some aspects that remind me of certain ancient Greek vases depicting the male nude."

Gwendolyn paused, "What's really curious are the faces. The woman is certainly Botticelli's Venus herself, but the Venus of your painting. She's almost like an ancient earth goddess from the primordial time when women were an integral part of procreation. A time when the line between a real woman and the Great Mother was blurred. Procreation was a holy act of devotion to the Life Force between the Sky God and the Earth Goddess. As for the faces of the men. They remind me of …"

"The Earth Mother! Yes, that's it! It never occurred to me before, but you nailed it." Rui nervously changed Gwendolyn's focus back onto the main character of his paintings, indeed the subject of his devotion. For the first time he understood his inspiration for the men in his paintings. He instinctively knew that was, in fact, embarrassing and did not need to hear her analysis of that.

"Gwendolyn, you are simply wonderful. The afternoon is slipping away. The sunlight is changing how we see the colors. I have many others with different styles and subjects that we can discuss another time. Perhaps tomorrow we can resume?

"If you agree, I would like to invite you to stay with me, I mean us, in the attic flat. That used to be my studio until climbing the stairs interfered with my desire to paint, to recreate the images that fill my mind. You can stay as long as you want. Wow! I'd have a genuine artist in residence. Please say yes! Or at least promise me you'll seriously consider it."

He sounds like a nervous teenager asking the girl of his dreams to the high school prom, Gwendolyn thought. She paused before answering.

Rui anxiously hastened to add: "Don't answer now. I must seem like a foolish teenager. But I'm very serious. I'll tell you what. I'll walk my dogs tomorrow morning as usual. At 0830 tomorrow I'll pass by the entrance of the Palacio Hotel. If I see you there, then wonderful. If not, well, I guess I'd understand. So, before I say something more to turn you off of the idea, I'll call a taxi to take you back to the hotel."

Gwendolyn's womanly instinct told her she had him, but that it would be a good ploy to play a little hard to catch. "OK, Rui. Let me think about it. I mean, after all, I only met you this morning. We artists are supposed to be such daring free spirits. Even so, I should pause before leaping. I'm not a teenager anymore. I don't need a taxi. It's only a five-minute walk."

"I'll walk you back."

"Now you're being silly, Rui. You can escort me to your impressive gate, and I can walk the rest of the way."

He led her slowly through the house as if he was soon to part with a treasure. He opened the front gate and with a pleading questioning voice, "Until tomorrow?"

"You'll just have to be surprised, Rui," she said with a wave as she started down the hill.

CHAPTER FIVE

Back in her hotel room, Gwendolyn called Giles.

"So, how did it go, little minx?"

"Oh, he was easy. Besides my choice of wardrobe, I purposely painted a yacht out of its true proportion. That certainly caught his professional interest. He had no choice but to correct me. What truly affected him was discovering that Venus, his beloved, shares my red hair. Or perhaps I should say, I share the same red hair as she does."

"So far, so good. Before we start, are you sure? If anything bothers you, we can stop right now."

"Nothing really, except the first morning I was painting, a strange sinister man accompanied Rui. He said something about how only goddesses should have red hair. All others should die. Can you imagine something so insane? I've not seen him since and hopefully never will again."

"Hm, that's crazy. I'll make a mental note and ask my contacts if they know who he is. What can you tell me about him?"

"He's thin and petite, with a full head of white hair. I'd guess he's the same age as Rui, somewhere in his mid-seventies. Spoke with an English accent. That's it, I think. Oh, and he walked with a slight limp."

"A slight limp with an English accent? OK. This will take some time, but I'll see what I can do. What about Rui?"

"He seems to me a kind, gentle soul at ease with himself and the world. Very easy going, I'd say."

"Sounds like he's a typical Portuguese. Anything else?"

"The only odd thing is he calls himself a devotee of Venus, the Goddess of Physical Love. Yet, he admits he is physically not up for it. So, it must be a Platonic thing. I doubt there's any danger of him becoming a devotee of me, though giving me some Platonic devotion would be fine, just enough to finish the painting. Although I confess there is something appealing about him. Nothing physical, mind you. It's his voice. So, to answer your question. Yes, I'm definitely up for this adventure."

"OK. Have you decided on a hotel yet? Will you stay at the Palacio? Tell me where to deliver your color analysis computer. Get me a sample of the frame, so we can start on reproducing that. Fortunately, we are doing the Birth of Venus and not Botticelli's other famous painting, Primavera (Spring). He painted that one on a wood panel. It would be much harder to find a 550-year-old wood panel of any size. Let's hope the frame it has is much more modern."

"I'll be able to tell you tomorrow. It certainly will not be the Palacio. I'm supposed to move out and into his attic apartment, remember? I'll look for an appropriate hotel a little further away. For now, I'll walk down to the beach and go for a swim. I'm as tightly wound up as a top."

"Don't bother finding a hotel. Let me do that. Expect a text message from me in an hour or so. You'll find the water is too cold for swimming. I don't want you to catch a cold."

"I need something bracing. Besides, the last time I was sick was close to twenty years ago. I choose not to get sick. It's a great waste of time."

"Like Voltaire choosing to be happy because it's good for his health?"

"I'm too young to be concerned with what's good for my health. Maybe I should be. In any case, I'm doing what I love."

"I'm doing the same. Let's start this ship's voyage!"

Gwendolyn entered the ocean's swells. The water was indeed too brisk to stay in long. It was not a seaside for leisurely bathing, but rather for swimming vigorously. All the surfers and scuba divers wore full body wetsuits. The sunset was astounding, but the quickly falling temperature compelled her to return to the Palacio.

Giles texted her: *I set you up in the deluxe bungalow at the Amazonia. You can check in tonight if you want.*

Following her shower, Gwendolyn walked three minutes to the other side of the casino and up the hill to check in at the Amazonia. Her bungalow faced south and the ocean letting in plenty of natural light. She stepped out onto the veranda and sank onto the soft sofa. She sighed in relief. With the preliminaries completed, she was ready to start a new adventure.

She realized she had read a novel a few years before, *Only After Dark*, written by one of her favorite authors, Thomas H Murray. The story took place in Estoril, precisely in the neighborhood surrounding her. She walked a minute or two to the palace of Carlos II, where the Romanian king lived in exile until his death. The condos underwent a full renovation since the story took place in the late 1970s, contrasting with the ruin described in the book.

Gwendolyn wandered through the largest casino in Europe. The bar in the Estoril Casino, where the gun smuggler, Le Petit, was usually ensconced, was still there. Exiting the casino, she walked across to the opposite side. Standing at the park's top, she gazed upon the rolling sea below. To the right was the famous Deck Bar, where the protagonist spent so much time. Gwendolyn decided that she simply must have dinner there under the great panoply of trees with some of the wonderful Alentejano wine that the protagonist loved so very much.

She felt like celebrating, but she made it an early night. She had to be up at the break of day and ready to meet Rui and his dogs the next morning. After a few hours of sleep, she suddenly sat bolt upright, anxious that Rui might change his mind. She left her bed and stepped onto the veranda. The full moon filled the night sky with its pale light, brimming with the mysterious possibility of an alternate reality.

The moonlight calmed her, reminding her that it was highly unlikely he would do so. Most probably, he was staring at the same moon at that very moment, anxious that she perhaps might not show up. She smiled at that and returned to bed, sleeping soundly until her cellphone alarm buzzed at 0630.

She had a full breakfast in the hotel garden. From where she sat, Gwendolyn could see through the lobby and out the front door. At 0810, he appeared, standing next to the doorman just outside, looking worried with his impatient dogs. She considered if she should put his anxiety to an end by meeting him right then or make him wait. She ordered another cappuccino. His anticipation would cause him to desire her company even more. But she was not mean and would meet him on time.

Much to his relief, at exactly 0830, the doorman opened the door, and she stepped outside. "Ah, Rui, so great to meet you on this beautiful day. As you can see, I've checked out. How are you? Did you sleep well?"

"Oh, Gwendolyn, I'm wonderful now that you accepted my offer. And no, I did not sleep well. But no matter, I'll sleep much better knowing I have you to discuss art with. I hope you can improve my own art with the critique of your professional help. You travel light. Here, let me take your bag."

"Please, Rui, I am not in the habit of others carrying my bags. Besides, you have five impatient dogs to handle. Shall we?"

"Oh, we shall, we shall." He said as he began the quick climb to his home and the lair of the strange Venus.

After entering the front gate with its rows of welcoming nymphs, Rui released his dogs into the garden. He opened the front door and welcomed her to enter. At the foot of the stairs, he grabbed one of her bags. Gwendolyn thought she should let him so as not to hurt his manly pride. But after barely making it to the floor of bedrooms with sweat pouring down his face, she gently took her bag back. After catching his breath, he smiled wanly and continued to lead her to the attic flat.

After a moment of wheezing, Rui managed to get out, "It's all yours for as long as you like. You can see the ocean from that window. I'll leave you to unpack and settle in. Join us in the sunroom for brunch when you're ready." With that he turned and left her alone.

Gwendolyn unpacked her bags and, as she placed her hand on the doorknob to go downstairs, she gasped at what caught the corner of her eye. There, hanging on the wall, was a photo of Rui and that terrible man who accompanied him on the first day of her painting. It was from when they were in their thirties. They clearly were very close friends, closer than friends it seemed to her. There was something strange in their expressions. Rui's face was rather vacuous. Despite the anger in his eyes, the other one was smiling sweetly. She removed the framed photo from the wall and headed downstairs.

There she found Rui and Luisa sitting with another royal brunch laid out between them in the garden sunroom. Having regained her composure, Gwendolyn asked, "Rui, is this how you eat every morning?"

"Yes, every morning. You know, we're supposed to eat breakfast like a king, lunch like a prince, and dinner like a pauper. But don't worry. Let's just say we dine like merchants, very successful ones. Please sit here, so you can view the blooming flowers in their full glory. This is your seat, the place of honor. What is that you have there?"

"Oh, this is a photo I found hanging on the wall in my room. When I was painting by the ocean five days ago, we saw each other for the first time. You were walking your dogs with a strange man. George, I believe that is what you called him. I heard him say the most awful things about redheads after he noticed me. The words he used, and the hateful sound of his voice make me shudder. I'm probably being silly, but if you don't mind, I'd rather not have this in my room."

"I'm so sorry you had to hear that. For over fifty years, George has been a very dear friend of mine. I've told him uncountable times to seek professional help. As you may have guessed from his accent, he is from an upper-class family of one of the lessor noble families of England. His mother was a redhead maid from Ireland, employed on the family estate. She caught his father's eye and, after the appropriate time, gave birth to George.

"During her pregnancy, she was locked out of sight in an abandoned hunting lodge in the forest behind the estate. Until the age of six, George lived with his mother. He adored her. I think worshiped her would be more accurate. Then came the time for his education. His father adopted him as his own and sent him away to a boarding school. While George was living at school, his father banished his mother back to Ireland with a generous stipend, as such things are usually done. That was the last he ever saw of her. It broke his heart. He never recovered.

"I'm not a psychologist, but I would venture to say that when he sees a redhead woman, he thinks of his mother and all that pain returns. The extreme anger and hatred of his father becomes focused on the poor redhead stranger. George has always had issues with women, but this is something way beyond that. But not to worry. To my knowledge, he has never harmed anyone, man or woman. And besides, he doesn't visit often. You most likely will not see him again. Luisa, dear, please take the photo and put it somewhere safe." He took the offending photo from Gwendolyn and handed it to her.

Luisa reacted as if Rui had suddenly put a snake in her face. Her face tightened into a grimace; her body instinctively recoiled. She refused to take it. Rui insisted, and finally she relented. "I'd rather put it on a fire. Why do you continue to associate with this god-cursed sodomite?"

"Now Luisa, you know he's one of my oldest friends. And that means a lot to me. If he tells me to throw you out, do you think I would listen?" He took her hand and gave a reassuring smile.

She rose and took the photo somewhere else. When she returned, Rui asked her where she put it. She had hidden it and refused to tell him. As a serious argument brewed, Gwendolyn came to the rescue by changing the subject.

"I'll have to learn the daily flow here. As it turns out, I already had my brunch at the Palacio. But I can always have more coffee." She sat in the offered chair and joined them. Being an excellent conversationalist, a necessary skill in her profession, a few hours quickly passed. Luisa sat stone-faced and said nearly nothing the whole time.

As the conversation wound to a close, Gwendolyn concluded, "Rui, you are so kind and generous. I don't ever wish for you to feel you're obligated. If you think I've become a bore or a burden, let me know and I'll leave. Anyway, obviously this is not a permanent solution to my new life in Portugal.

She paused briefly, allowing Luisa to breathe a sigh of relief, and then resumed speaking. "I will help you with your painting and we can talk about art all you want. I must take time to find my own place. Around eight hours a day should suffice, perhaps during the time between brunch and dinner. In that way, you can pursue your own activities, like painting, while I enjoy a leisurely walk after this delicious brunch.

"Gwendolyn, you'd never be a bore or a burden. That simply is not possible. I can help you find a place to live. I could place a few phone calls now and you'd have a place before dinner, rent-free, too."

"Thank you for your kind offer, Rui. I have no doubt you could easily do that. But I want my own place. I need to always maintain my independence. So, I must refuse your thoughtful gesture. In any case, I'll start tomorrow. Let's discuss art this afternoon and maybe show me more of your paintings. Are you working on one now?"

"Fine. I respect your independence, but if you ever need any help with anything, you must let me know. Agreed?"

"Agreed, Rui. So, what is your plan for today?"

"I'll show you what I'm currently doing. Let's go to my studio." As a diplomatic afterthought, he added, "Would you care to join us, Luisa?"

She did for not quite twenty minutes and then became bored and left. She sat on a lounge chair in the garden reading a collection of poems by Sophia de Mello Breyner Andresen, keeping the studio in view.

Gwendolyn noted her interest in poetry, something they had in common. She would use that later to discover the path through her defensiveness and disarm her doubts. Luisa was obviously an educated woman. But with no marketable skills and midway through her fifties, she easily fell prey to her insecurities. She had come to rely on an eccentric man for her life, a man she barely understood. Then, out of the blue enters a young woman into their home, threatening to upset everything. Gwendolyn would need to handle this with care.

After brunch, Rui retired to his study to handle whatever business and other matters he had. Doing anything serious at a desk quickly drained him. He had an hour-long siesta before he took his dogs for a late afternoon walk. Luisa made the most of this time to take care of the house and run errands.

As Gwendolyn settled into the tranquility of the garden, she delved into a collection of essays on the theory of aesthetics by Su Shi, an artist, calligrapher, poet, and art theorist of China's Song dynasty (960 to 1279). She read it in the original classical Chinese, having learned that magnificent language during her earlier years of researching Asian art in Taiwan. After deciding she was a friend of the family, the resident canines lounged around her feet.

She waited until the house was silent. Rui was taking his nap and Luisa was out doing errands. She entered the living room and sat before the great painting that she would understand intimately before she moved on to her next professional project. She took out her device that could detect any electronics in the room, including security cameras. There were none.

Next, she pulled out her small, sharp, spring-activated device to collect a sample of the wooden frame and its paint. She could extract this tiny wooden shard from where no one would notice, except with a strong magnifying glass. Even then, the hole was no larger than what a small wood boring insect would make.

Finally, she photographed the painting with a special camera the size of a cellphone—in fact, it was made to look like one. But this camera took extremely high-resolution digital photos. Gwendolyn would later download these images into her highly specialized computer that Giles would so kindly set up in her bungalow studio. The computer would analyze the colors and the layers of paint, allowing her to reproduce the exact pigments and methods of the great artist himself.

After returning to her place in the shade under the garden trees, she texted Giles: *So far, everything fine. Meet me tomorrow at 14   00. Have the thing you want.* Gwendolyn always texted him somewhat cryptically as she did not want anyone to read her text messages secretly and find anything incriminating. Ten minutes later, while she was reading about the changes that pine trees go through in each season, He responded: *K!*

After a relatively light meal concluded by 21   00, Rui and Gwendolyn retired to the living room, settling themselves in below the wanton gaze of the mysterious Venus. Rui greatly appreciated his Portuguese wine. She had no intention of even trying to keep up. Two glasses of wine were enough for her. Rui drank at least a bottle at dinner and nearly half a bottle of old port wine, staring into the eyes of his true love. Perhaps he hoped she would reignite the passion she promised her adherents. But with every sip of port wine, that hope became ever more elusive.

By 2300, he was asleep in his chair. Luisa entered soon afterwards and helped him to bed. Gwendolyn, for her part, retired to hers. As she lay in bed, the silver light of the moon filled the room and bathed her in its cool glow. The blank spot on the wall where the objectionable picture hung brought back the image of the crazy George. She hung her recently finished painting of the sea and its corrected yacht there. With a calmer mind, she sank onto the pillow more relaxed.

Gwendolyn turned on her side and studied the moon filling the night sky through the opened window. Before sleep could drop its diaphanous veil over her mind, she considered her situation. She had successfully passed through her first day and learned the daily schedule of the odd couple. It was a schedule she could work with.

She fell asleep, impatient to get started.

CHAPTER SIX

The next morning, after their late brunch, Gwendolyn announced that she would start her search for a place to live. First, she had to decide on the area, somewhere between Cascais and Lisboa, close to the light rail and the water. Rui was a bit distracted.

As she approached the front gate, Luisa called to her. She turned around to face the unexpected greeting. Luisa held out a set of keys. "Here. You'll want these to come and go as you like."

As she reached to take them, Gwendolyn said gently, "You know, I am no threat to you at all. I intend to move out as soon as possible. Besides, we have several things in common. We both love poetry and we both hate misogynist men."

Luisa smiled and pressed Gwendolyn's hand in both of hers. "Just remember, things aren't what they seem here. Pray that George never shows up while you're here. He's more than just a strange twit. How I loathe him! But let's stay positive. Have a good day house hunting."

At that moment, Rui called for her from the open front door. "Gotta go. We'll see you for dinner." She released Gwendolyn's hands and entered the house.

Gwendolyn walked down the hill towards the Estoril train station, but at the Casino, she turned right for the Amazonia Hotel. This small hotel with its curvy Art Deco exterior perches at the crest of a hill a five-minute walk from the beach. There are two parts. The main hotel with the reception lies at the top of a gated driveway for short-term stays.

The other part separated by trees and a garden contains individual bungalows for longer-term stays, each containing a kitchen, a living room, and a private veranda. They are nearly hidden from each other by flowers, bushes, and palm trees. Guests could also enter the bungalows from an unmarked metal door on a different street than the main gate. A tall ivory-covered wall surrounded the metal door that opened from the sidewalk. It was perfect for discrete entrances and exits.

After checking in to her bungalow studio, she texted Giles that she had arrived. He immediately replied that he would be there in an hour with her color analysis computer. She told him she would meet him at the train station, sitting just above the beach, and help him carry the things he brought. She passed Estoril's Institute of the Misericórdia (mercy), founded by Queen Leonor de Viseu in 1498, as a charitable organization to aid those who could use a good dose of mercy in their lives.

The gate stood   open, and she had time to investigate. It was housed in an Art Deco mansion built by a successful engineer in the 1930s, surrounded by a spacious garden of statues and fountain-fed ponds shaded by towering old trees. What interested Gwendolyn was that they offered very reasonably priced classes across a wide range of subjects, mainly geared to the retired Portuguese, but they also had Portuguese language classes for foreigners.

In the end, she decided not to take Portuguese lessons. She did not want any distractions and, besides, she had misgivings about living so near to the scene of her crime. Perhaps she would return to live in Portugal when she retired in forty or fifty years. But by then, the world would be a different place with different choices.

She passed the remaining time, seated by a tall stone pillar at the end of a jetty jutting into the Atlantic Ocean. The waves crashing with their regular rhythm on the rocks below gave her a feeling of serenity. Giles arrived on time in disguise, looking like a young Bohemian French painter complete with beret and a roll of canvas in a long, thick tube under his arm instead of a baguette. His bushy black mustache really needed a trim. Gwendolyn greeted him in French and took the heavy wooden box of pigments and paints he was struggling with.

Giles responded, "Allons-y, ma chérie."

"Ah, a poet, too?"

"Yes, I'm a poet and I don't even know it. I come up with a rhyme every time."

"Oh, you silly man. This way."

In her bungalow, they laid everything out. She set up her extendable easel to its full extent. Giles helped her unroll the canvas and secure it on the period appropriate wooden stretchers he brought. They placed the two-meter canvas on the easel that barely missed the nine-meter/yard ceiling. That activity alone took nearly two hours.

She handed him her device with the wood sample from Botticelli's frame. He set up her computer on an out-of-the-way desk. She inserted her camera's chip so it could download the image and do

45

its color analysis. While they waited for this lengthy process, she prepared her workspace by laying out the period paints and brushes, each in their proper place. Giles opened a bottle of wine, found two glasses in the bungalow's kitchen, and prepared a plate of cheese and olives on the veranda.

"Come, dearie, and enjoy the wonderful view of the ocean. This is Portugal, where everything takes longer, and life is to be enjoyed. The computer needs time to do its thing anyway."

"Ah, a place after my own heart. I'll never say 'no' to enjoying life."

"Speaking of enjoying life, when will you find your special man? I've already found mine in Lisboa."

"Giles, I thought we were talking about enjoying life. The last thing I need is to be tied down by some possessive, demanding boy-man. If I need a temporary diversion, there's never a shortage of eye candy to be found."

"I prefer man-boys myself. But fine, let's change the subject. How are things in Estoril?"

Gwendolyn reviewed the events of the past few days, including more regarding the strange sinister George and Luisa's reaction to the photo. Giles sipped slowly from his glass before voicing any opinion.

"Clearly, you haven't lost your touch. Rui was even easier than I thought. Seems like you have an open invitation to stay as long as you want now that you have eased the natural suspicions Luisa had. This is an exceptionally large painting. You'll need more time than normal to complete it."

"Yes, but I still think I can finish it in about two and a half, maybe three months, max. I can think of better places to sleep than in a dusty attic in the home of an eccentric old man. But what's your thoughts on George?"

"Ah, George… I really have no opinion other than to avoid him. I haven't been able to discover anything about him yet. I'll continue with my search. In any case, you're a better judge than me. Hopefully, he'll not turn up again."

"I'd say he definitely is sinister. I'd rather not find out whether he's harmless or not. Another reason not to delay. Speaking of which, sounds like the computer has stopped its analysis. Let's take a look at the results, shall we?"

Gwendolyn sat down in front of the computer. Giles pulled up a chair and sat beside her. After a half an hour of careful study of the data, she pushed her chair back and looked at her questioning partner.

"Hm, interesting, very interesting. There exist several significant differences from the well-known one. First, Botticelli painted Rui's version on a single piece of canvas, whereas he painted the famous one on two sewn together. This base coat gesso has more of a green tint than the other. This gives the flesh tones a unique effect.

"In the version Botticelli created for the Medici's, he covered over a few details that he thought it would be better without. But here he kept them. For example, Flora on the right has sandals in this one. Botticelli painted over them in the other. The robe Flora is holding out for Venus has no mantle, but in the Uffizi version he added it in later. Also, the greens and the blues have become darker over the years. I'll need to take that into account.

"Botticelli used an egg yolk varnish on the Medici version, but on this one he used a litharge varnish made from lead monoxide, walnut oil, and white beeswax. It's a hassle to make. I hope you have the right specialists to do it. I don't have the patience."

"Let me handle all the technical issues. What else?"

"The most obvious difference is that all three women figures have darker red hair, closer to mine. Those are the key differences regarding color and paint. I already explained the variances in the composition. You can see them for yourself."

"Yes, they do have the same red hair as you. Interesting… Hm, well, I'll let you get to it. I'll give you the varnish and the frame before you need them. It's time for me to leave. I have an important date tonight. No need to take up your time. I can make it back to the train station on my own. Let me know if you need anything."

"Fine, Giles. Don't forget to tell me if you learn anything more about this strange George. Will talk soon."

Gwendolyn spent the rest of the afternoon studying the artist's style, the painting's composition, its various layers, and colors. Then she stared at the blank canvas, pondering her strategy. As the sun's rays began to wane, she turned off the computer and locked it to the desk by wrapping a steel cable around the desktop. To steal the computer, a thief would need to saw the desk in half. Even in the third safest country in the world, one could not be too careful.

She detoured to the beach to admire the golden sunset over the Cascais harbor and the Atlantic Ocean. She had a glass of white wine at one of the beachside cafés. The sun felt good holding her in his gentle arms. Walking back to Rui's house in the twilight, she asked herself the perennial question that would sometimes pop up in her mind. When would she start creating her own paintings and develop her own art career? She gave herself her usual answer: when she had enough money saved from her special projects. But how much was enough? She never had an answer for that one.

Dinner with Rui and Luisa was a very quiet affair. They must have quarreled during the day. Gwendolyn thought she could guess over what. But that suited her fine. She was more interested in mulling over the painting that occupied her mind. Despite more wine than usual, Rui could not quite muster up his normal joviality.

After dinner, they sat before the fireplace as was now their custom, staring in silence at the wonderful wanton Venus enticing them from above. Rui steadily drank his port until he fell asleep in his chair. Luisa helped him to bed, leaving Gwendolyn alone with Venus. With a magnifying glass in hand, she meticulously examined the painting for over an hour.

Finally, she sat back down with a sigh. Poured herself a glass of Rui's port wine and smiled. Capturing the painting's spirit was essential to reproducing it. This required many hours of simply taking it all in. Each time, another aspect would present itself. The more she studied the painting the more confident she became that she could reproduce it in painstaking detail.

She closed her eyes and imagined that she was floating in the same calm waters that gave birth to the famous goddess with her offer of universal physical pleasure, so important for alleviating the misery of life. Her mind drifted further. She slowly transferred herself into being the great goddess displaying her full glory surrounded by nymphs and a wind god softly blowing her to shore with his flower-scented breath.

She finished her glass and rose to go to sleep. Tomorrow she would put paint to canvas and start the daunting task before her.

CHAPTER SEVEN

The next day's late afternoon sun spread its warm glow throughout the bungalow studio. Gwendolyn was just finishing spreading the green-tinted gesso across the entire 500-year-old canvas that would form the base coat. She took a seat to inspect her work and liked what she saw. She often wondered where Giles found all the art materials of the correct age for whatever painting she had to reproduce.

Thinking of him, she picked up her cellphone that she always had on vibrate to check if he had called. She was too engrossed in her painting to notice that indeed he had called her. She phoned back.

"You called?"

"Yes. I figured you must have been too deeply concentrating to hear me. Listen, have you been keeping up with the news?"

"No, Giles. You know I never 'keep up' with the news. My life wraps around 500-year-old art. Has the world ended yet?"

"No, not for most people, anyway. There's some shocking news coming out of Italy today, Florence specifically. Apparently, there is a sick serial killer lurking there. The police have linked the murders of seventeen young women over the past four years to a single culprit. The victims all share three things in common.

"They had all visited the Uffizi Museum. They all were decapitated. And they all were redheads. I think it would be safe to add a fourth thing. They had all probably seen Botticelli's The Birth of Venus."

"No, no, I haven't heard about that. And you're telling me this because?"

"Because? Because you have red hair and you're just starting to reproduce his other Venus. You're intimately connected to her. Gwendolyn, I have a bad feeling about this. Maybe you should stop this project."

"A bad feeling? Why? I'm not even in Italy. Seems the killer is stalking the halls of the Uffizi, not the quiet lanes of Estoril. Yes, I have red hair, but so what? Giles, sometimes you're…" She suddenly paused. "Wait a minute! You're not thinking that the killer might be George? Giles, that's a bit of a leap even for you."

"OK, look, I may be overreacting, but I'd rather be safe than sorry. Please stop the painting and return to Lisboa. We have plenty of other projects to do."

"No, Giles. I'm completely engaged with this. I've already started, and I must admit, I'm becoming somewhat obsessed with it. Sometimes I imagine that I'm the very same Venus. Somehow, I feel as if I'll be painting myself. Besides, I'm growing rather fond of the old eccentric Rui."

"Jeez, Gwendolyn, I'm telling you it's simply not worth the risk. This is the first time I have lost my normal cheery self-confidence about a project. Look, at least dye your hair some other color."

"Dye my hair some other color? Are you crazy? I would never do that. Besides, it seems that part of my attraction to Rui is indeed my beautiful red hair. Yes, clearly, I'm a redhead, I'm painting a Botticelli, and, yes, George is a creep. But I'm not in Florence and I'm not painting that Botticelli. What I'm painting might not even be one of his for all we know. Relax. Everything will turn out fine."

The phone was silent for a moment before he exhaled slowly. "OK, if you're so sure. You're closer to the situation than me. But please be careful. Lock your door at night. Be wary of anyone following you. Tell me the second you feel uncomfortable. Can you promise me that?"

"Y-e-s, Uncle Giles, I promise. I want to catch the sunset by the beach before dinner. I'll talk to you later." She hung up.

Gwendolyn put everything away, made sure she locked the door, and walked the short distance down the hill to the busy coastal road known as the Marginal. There she passed below through the tunnel under the train station and out to the incredible blue sea under the equally blue sky, all awash in the golden blaze of the setting sun. She sat on the nearby concrete ledge and marveled at the astonishing beauty displayed.

The walkway immediately in front of her was the Paredão busy with people enjoying the last few hours of sunlight, walking their dogs, jogging, or only ambling along. On the other side of this display of humanity lay the beach with the Atlantic Ocean beyond. Basking in the sun's warm embrace, she shut her eyes and sighed.

Slowly, an uncomfortable feeling entered the peaceful meditations of her mind. She ignored it at first, but it only grew stronger. Someone was watching her. She opened her eyes and, exactly as her feelings revealed, there was indeed a man about ten meters to her right, staring at her. The setting sun's glare behind him prevented her from clearly seeing his details.

He lifted both his hands in a thumbs up gesture. Then he made a sound. What was it? He was laughing, but not in joy. Gwendolyn's heart froze. It was the maniacal laughter of madness. He was nodding at her. That was too much. Though nothing was clear between the distance and the sun, she decided it was time to go.

As she rose to leave, so did he. He was closing the distance. Entering the tunnel, she noticed his shadow stretching in front of her. Hearing the train approach the station above, she ran up the stairs and onto the train right as the doors were shutting. She had no ticket but would prefer to brave the ticket checker than whomever it was she left on the station platform, rapidly fading away behind.

Gwendolyn sighed in relief. Before she could begin to carefully analyze what had recently occurred, the train slowed as it approached the next stop. She hopped out before the train took her too far away. Her cellphone's GPS told her she had a half an hour walk to the safe haven behind the locked gate of Rui's home. Walking along the narrow streets of Estoril, she slowly unwound from whatever it was exactly that she had just experienced.

He was without a doubt strange, his attention clearly distressing. Calmer now, she asked herself, was he different from any of the other unpleasant attention from vaguely threatening men that women receive nearly every day? She started to believe he was only that. He probably heard the train he wanted to catch, but just narrowly missed it, as she nearly did.

Had it been George? That question burned in her mind. She could not be sure. The sunlight prevented her from seeing his face clearly. Giles seemed to think he was in Florence, cutting down red-headed adoring Botticelli fans. His phone call must have spooked her more than she thought. She laughed at the absurdity of it all and let that weight of anxiety fall from her shoulders. Her footsteps returned to their normal light saunter.

Gwendolyn decided she really needed to get a grip. Why did she panic so quickly? She could have continued through the tunnel to the Deck Bar on the other side, sat under the trees, sipping a glass of wine, and watched what that strange man did. Well, alas, she did not do that, but in any case, she was approaching the place she called home for the moment.

She had checked frequently to make sure no one was following her. She did the same before she unlocked the gate. The street remained empty. Laughing at herself, she entered Rui's house. With an hour before dinner, Gwendolyn made up her mind to have a good soak in a warm bath. With her limbs stretched under the soapy water of a bubble bath, she shut her eyes and relaxed.

About ten minutes later, she heard the wheeze and heavy breathing of someone struggling up the stairs. It continued outside her door. There was a light knock shortly before the door opened and   in came Rui.

"Rui, I could hear your heavy breathing before you even reached my door. If you want to sneak into my room while I'm taking a bath, you'll have to get in better shape than that." She swung the bathroom door shut with a slam.

"So sorry, but I knocked, you know."

"You call that a knock? What do you want? What's so important that it couldn't wait until dinner?"

"I'd rather not shout through a closed door. Can you come out? I'll close my eyes."

"Close your eyes?" She laughed. "I have a bathrobe here. No need to be so ridiculous." She quickly dried herself and put on her robe.

She opened the door and sat on the chair by the window. "OK. What is so important? Are you throwing me out?"

"Throwing you out? No, no, I would never consider doing that. Throwing you out is the furthest from my mind. I have some disturbing news. I don't enjoy discussing unpleasant things while Luisa is present. She's the sensitive kind. I don't know if you've heard about what's happening in Florence?"

"Florence? You mean about the murders of the redheads? Yeah, I've already heard about that. Do you have something new to add? Do you know who the murderer is? Is he here in Estoril?" Her pulse rose again.

"No, no, Gwendolyn, I have nothing else to say other than please be careful. There are a lot of crazies out there. Sorry to disturb you. I'll see you soon for dinner, yes?"

"Thanks for your concern. I'll be down in ten minutes."

Rui left her, returning downstairs. She considered this strange encounter. The first thing that entered her mind was kicking herself for not following Giles' advice about locking her door. Her second thought was that Rui apparently did not think it was George. Finally, she smiled at how sweet it was for him to struggle up the stairs to warn her of a far-off fear.

She dressed herself and went downstairs. Despite all her rational explanations, she still felt rattled. To help her unwind, she decided to partake of Rui's port wine after dinner. Otherwise, it would be a long night staring at the passing moonlight too wired to sleep. She had a painting she needed to do with a clear, well-rested mind.

The meal was excellent and the conversation stimulating. After dinner, while sitting by the captivating Venus, the port wine flowed smoothly. It was doing what it did best. She relaxed as the tension of the day melted away. Before she knew it, the grandfather clock in the corner struck 2300. That was the signal for Luisa to enter silently and help the already slumbering Rui to bed. Gwendolyn followed soon after.

She smiled as she remembered to lock the door behind her. In bed, she pulled the covers over her, turned on her side, and fell at once to sleep. Even so, the day's nervous events still had to play themselves out in her dreams.

In the darkness of night, she was walking along a narrow trail in a thick jungle, perhaps the Amazon. The moon shone down from above, illuminating her way. Vines and branches beside the trail were reaching for her, touching her as she passed.

In the treetops above her, many spider monkeys cast their shadows on her as they flitted through the branches under the moonlight. They squawked at her threateningly. Their dark shapes changed. From normal sized spider monkeys, they became giant monkey spiders. She screamed and ran as the dark silhouettes encircled her, embraced her.

She came upon a clearing and tripped on a root. Sprawled under the moon's bright light, the shadows of the forest retreated. She looked up at the savior moon with relief. Suddenly, a larger threatening shadow flew above her, blocking out the moon like an eclipse in reverse.

Trying to force herself awake to end the nightmare, she could only open her eyes halfway. A large dark figure squatted on its haunches in her open bedroom window, blocking the moon. Its shadow fell upon her. She woke completely and sat up in bed. With her eyes wide open now, and her heart pounding, she realized nothing was lurking in her empty open window.

Regaining control of her breath, she rose, closed the window and its curtain. *What the hell, Gwendolyn? Get a hold of yourself!* She returned to bed and noticed it was only 0315. That really annoyed her more than the nightmare. She still had four hours left to get her full eight hours of sleep. She lay back down, gazing at the now darkened ceiling above her.

The night slipped by. The rays of the sun peeking in through the hastily closed curtain woke her. In the end, she had her eight hours of sleep. She rubbed her eyes and smiled. Shaking off the dregs of her unpleasant nightmare, she rose to start her day.

CHAPTER EIGHT

Joyful that the disturbing images of the night before were only a nightmare, Gwendolyn skipped down the stairs to brunch. Her infectious joy perked up the gloomy Rui and Luisa. Soon everyone was in a chattier mood. The food proved as magnificent as ever. The lighter ambience made the important breaking of the nightly fast something to be relished. Even Luisa joined the conversation.

The painting's gesso base would need another full day to dry. Gwendolyn decided to take a break and pass the time more leisurely. She turned to Rui, "You know, Rui. I didn't sleep so well last night. Before you say anything, it had nothing to do with the wonderful bed and room. No, it was simply silly bad dreams. Maybe all this talk about the murders of redheads or who knows what else is causing them.

"So, if you don't mind, I found an English translation of Bernard Soares' The Book of Disquiet on your living room bookshelf. I think the Portuguese name is…" She butchered the word 'Desassossego'.

Luisa came to the rescue and pronounced it correctly and slowly, so Gwendolyn could learn how to say it.

"Thank you, Luisa. If it's not a problem, I'll take the day off from my search and find a cozy nook in your peaceful garden to read for today."

"Not a problem at all. You know you're welcome to stay here as long as you like." Luisa threw him a sharp look.

Rui noticed but ignored her. "Take as much time as you need to find your place. A dear friend gave me that book as a going away present when I left the UK finally to return to live in Portugal. It will take you the whole week or more to finish it. Too bad you can't read it in the original Portuguese. Allow me to say a few words on the subject.

"First, Bernard Soares is one of many heteronyms that Fernando Pessoa used. It's not a pen name. Each heteronym has his own personality, world outlook, style, etc. Of course, Soares is a creation of Pessoa. The book is very much a random collection of autobiographical musings. We can learn a lot about him personally by reading it.

"Second, it was not published until forty-seven years after he died in 1935. Pessoa wrote them on scraps of paper, backs of envelopes, etc. that they later found all mixed together in a large trunk. We can only guess the order of these musings, as there is no plot or logical progression that can help. It's most likely that he never meant them to be published. But published they are and has become one of the great canons of world literature, cementing his place as the greatest modern Portuguese poet." Rui was almost breathless when he finished.

"Wow! Thank you for that introduction. Now I definitely must read the whole thing. And I just chose it because of the English name, The Book of Disquiet. It's quite long. It'll probably take me a while."

"Read it for as long as you like. You know what? Take it. It's yours."

"Oh, Rui, this must mean a lot to you. I'm sure I can find it in a bookstore or even on Amazon."

"No, no, I insist. Besides, I don't trust just any translator. A fellow American from the US, Richard Zenith, a famous Pessoa scholar who lives in Lisboa translated this. He won the Pessoa Prize around ten years ago. He wrote a widely recognized biography about our poet. Now I must say…"

Luisa interrupted him. "Rui, is it really necessary to expound on this? I'm sure Gwendolyn does not need to understand every aspect of Pessoa's personal life to enjoy his poetry."

"Luisa, this is not just any aspect of his life. It's a vital one." Rui's voice rose.

She rolled her eyes, abruptly rose, noisily grabbed the dirty, empty plates, and left in a huff.

Rui continued, "Richard Zenith thinks Pessoa was probably gay. Probably gay? Pessoa wrote extensively about a fervent love he had for a young woman who we know as Ofélia Queirós. Because of his own complex, inward-focused poetic personality, it never bloomed into marriage. It was an on-again off-again relationship as Pessoa would swing from passionate love to passionate pain from a minor trifle that she said or didn't say, did or didn't do. Gays don't do that with women.

"He wrote many poems extolling blonds with silk scarves. In any case, the style of his poetry is not a 'gay' one. Believe me. I know what 'gay' poetry is, having been a part of that culture and lifestyle.

There was a time when I was very much into this genre. I suppose I was seeking reinforcement and even inspiration from it."

"Gay poets? Hm, I wonder if I know them. Give me some names."

"Besides the obvious ones like Oscar Wilde and your Alan Ginsberg and James Baldwin, there are others such as Dennis Cooper, Arthur Rimbaud, Frederico Lorca, Frank O'Hara, etc."

"I've heard that one of our greatest poets, Walt Whitman, was of that persuasion. But I've read his Leaves of Grass numerous times. He writes how he loves everyone and everything, in every sense of the word. It was also obvious from many of his poems that he very much enjoyed the physical comfort and pleasures of women."

"Ah, Whitman! Now there's a man with a heart as big as his country. Pessoa didn't like his poetry. Of course, they are as different as imaginable. Pessoa had a heart for others as small as his country. He lived in his mind whereas Whitman lived in all the world. Dare I say, beyond the world, reaching to the greatest heights man has ever pushed beyond his mind. We cannot say he was a gay poet. His poetry transcends the world and all its labels. We could call him today 'bisexual' or even that new word 'pansexual'."

"OK, Rui. I think I got it. Thanks for the background. I'll just dive in and see where it takes me." She rose from her chair.

Rui held her arm. "I wonder if you can help me. I mean us really." Gwendolyn sat back down.

"Sure. What is it?"

"Luisa has been very touchy lately. I think I know what's bothering her."

"Oh, I know. It must be me. Am I doing anything untoward?"

"No, no, of course not. And neither have I, have I?"

Gwendolyn stayed silent as she remembered him coming into her room while she was in the bathtub. "How can I help?"

"You seem to have much knowledge and interest in poetry. It's Luisa's passion. She'll probably be in the garden today reading her favorite poetry. Perhaps you could find a way to use that angle to encourage her not to be so defensive and sensitive. Help her accept you, not as a rival or even as a friend. Maybe something in between might be the best we can hope for."

"Fine, Rui. I'll keep an eye open for an opportunity to do so today."

Rui sat back and sighed in relief. "Thank you. We'll talk later."

Gwendolyn rose, grabbed her book of disquiet, and found her favorite spot to read. About fifteen minutes later, Luisa came into view, sitting at her preferred divan in the shade with a book in hand. After an hour of reading, her eyes needed a rest, though she found Pessoa's poetry fascinating.

As Rui mentioned, she did learn several personal aspects of the great man. For example, he always ate dinner at the same restaurant in Lisboa at the same hour, precisely 1930, early by local standards. He preferred bananas from the Portuguese island of Madeira, despite normally having black spots on the skin. He liked taking the coastal train from Lisboa to Cascais.

She decided it was time to saunter over to Luisa and try to charm her into at least neutral territory. "Hello, Luisa. Another beautiful day in Portugal. Oh, I see you're reading the poetry of Sophia de Mello Breyner Andresen. She's my favorite Portuguese poet, after Fernando Pessoa, of course."

"Your favorite Portuguese poet after Fernando Pessoa? Oh, really? What do you know of her poetry? Did you see her name on the spine of one of my books on the same bookshelf where you found Pessoa's book? You'll have to do better than that to impress me." Luisa sneered, preparing to let her latent anger out on the source of her distrust and insecurity.

"A fair question. You must find it difficult to believe that a young girl from the US would know anything about Portuguese poetry. Well, you've now met one. Unfortunately, I cannot read the poetry in its original Portuguese. That's my bad. But read it I have.

"As for Sophia de Mello Breyner Andresen, I particularly love her 'On Crete'. It's a wonderful poem written when she traveled there in 1970, I believe it was. I don't remember the whole thing, but I do remember the final part:

"In Crete the brick walls of the Minoan city

Are made of clay kneaded with seaweed

And when I turned behind my shadow,

I saw that the sun touching my shoulder was blue.

In Crete, where the Minotaur reigns, I crossed the wave

With my eyes open and fully awake,

No drugs and no filter

Only wine drunk in front of the solemnity of things -

Because I belong to the race of those who walk the labyrinth,

Without ever losing the linen thread of the word."

A sad single tear trickled down Luisa's face. She closed her eyes and recited the beginning part that Gwendolyn could not remember:

"In Crete

Where the Minotaur reigns

I bathed in the sea

There's a quick dance you do in front of a bull

In the ancient youth of the day

No drug intoxicated me, hid me, protected me

I only drank retsina, having spilled on earth the part that belongs to the gods

Of Crete

I adorned myself with flowers and chewed the bitter herbs

To commune with the earth fully awake

From Crete

I kissed the ground like Ulysses

I walked in the naked light

Devastated was I myself like the ruined city

That no one rebuilt

But in the sun of my empty courtyards,

Fury reigns intact

And penetrates with me into the sea

Because I belong to the race of those who

dive with open eyes

And recognize the abyss stone by stone anemone by anemone flower by flower

And the sea of Crete inside is all blue

An incredible offering of primordial joy

Where the dark Minotaur sails

Paintings of waves, columns and plains

In Crete

Fully awake, I went through the day

And walked inside the vehement, red palaces

successive and hoarse palaces

Where the breath of whispered darkness rises,

And half-blue pupils of penumbra and terror stare at us

Immanent to the day -

I walked in the dual palace of combat and confrontation

Where the Prince of Lilies raises his morning gestures,

No drug has intoxicated me, hidden me, protected me

The Dionysos who dances with me on the wave is not sold on any black market

But grows like the flower of those whose being

Endlessly seek and loses itself and disunites and reunites

And this is the dance of being."

She remained silent for a moment. Suddenly, she jumped up and hugged Gwendolyn.

"Oh, my dear girl! That is exactly my favorite poem. How did you guess? Not even Rui understands the deepest feelings in my heart. You and I, we are kindred spirits, after all. I was so wrong about you. Can you forgive me?"

"What's there to forgive? I should ask you to forgive me for causing tension in this home. But that is the furthest from my intention. If it would make you feel better, I will leave now. Just give me the word."

"No, don't give it another thought. It's my own silly insecurities to blame. I see now that we are of the same race as Sophia Breyner Andresen. We might as well be sisters. You're welcome to stay here as long as you like. Here, sit next to me and we'll read our poetry together." She slid over to make space for Gwendolyn.

She sat beside her and opened her copy of Pessoa's Book of Disquiet. Rui watched them through the sunroom window and smiled.

CHAPTER NINE

The next morning, Gwendolyn leapt out of bed, excited finally to start her painting in earnest. She tried not to appear eating her morning meal too hurriedly. Despite her best efforts, Rui picked up on it.

"I trust you slept very well. You seem to be brimming with energy this morning."

"Yes, in fact, I did sleep well. Unusual for me, I slept straight through the night. I guess I'm just impatient to start my search for my future home."

"Well, don't let us hold you back."

"I think I can wait until after another cup of coffee."

She hurried to her bungalow studio with a spring in her step. She could hardly wait to return to doing what she loves best: painting.

During the five minutes it took to arrive, her mind raced, considering her next step on the path to completing her masterpiece.

Because the weekends and the weekdays held no difference in Rui's home, Gwendolyn painted on the weekends, too. After many weeks, the painting was coming together. She had painted all the principal forms and Botticelli's strange sea with its little eddies for waves. All that remained was to fill in all the details, which was the most important part.

One thing remained the same. She enjoyed her long port wine infused after-dinner conversations with Rui sitting in front of the very thing she obsessed over all her waking hours — and many of her sleeping hours, too. Gradually, Rui spoke more of his own painting, including technique, colors, and composition. He studiously avoided any mention of the subjects, instinctively considering them perhaps a bit too personal to be open to any criticism.

Gwendolyn could only speak in generalities, as they were not in front of the paintings. Rui clearly wanted her to spend more time with him in his studio. She had to swerve away from anything that would take her away from her own painting. Yet she knew Rui considered her as his personal in-house art critique and consultant to improve his painting, being one of her key attractions to living with them. She knew she would have to make time for him, no matter how distasteful trying to improve his strange paintings might be.

One evening in front of the fireplace, Rui was strangely silent, clearly mulling over something important. He made several attempts to start a conversation that would lead to the destination he had in mind, but words were failing him. Gwendolyn picked up on his nervousness and became nervous herself. Was he trying to find the words to ask her to leave? She regretted not carving out a half a day to help his art. She could only wait for him to find his bearings.

Eventually, after circling the subject in various obscure ways, he forced himself to come to the point. "Gwendolyn, I would like to ask you a favor. If you refuse, I'd understand. I'd think nothing less of you…. Look at me. I'm as tongue-tied as a teenaged boy asking for something that is so out of reach. What I mean to say is…." He fell back into silence.

"Well, Rui, what is it? I'll probably agree. But let me hear it first." She felt better now that the strange line of conversation did not appear to be leading to her having to leave before she had finished her project. What a waste that would be!

"OK, look, we're both artists, right? We're free spirits, not like other people, right? We'd do almost anything for our art. It's our passion, after all!"

He fell silent again. "I agree, Rui. Indeed, it is. Now out with it, man! What is it you want to ask?"

Rui took a deep breath and blurted out, "I want you to be my model, to pose for me as my personal Venus rising from the depths, just like Botticelli's Venus here on the wall."

"Is that what this is all about?"

"Yes." He mumbled, "But I want you to do it in the nude, just like the original."

"Did I hear you correctly? You want me to do it in the nude?"

"Yes. In the nude. P-p-please at least consider it b-b-before you say no. If you don't want to, then we'll just forget that I ever brought it up." Rui's nervous voice almost cracked.

"Wow, Rui. Really? I must think this one over a bit. I'll let you know before the weekend. You'll have to assure me that there would be no problem with Luisa. Now let's change the subject. I think we were last discussing the pre-Raphaelites."

Rui was relieved that she did not slap him and immediately move out. At least there was a possibility. Of course, he was attracted to her as any man would be. Yet, he really did want to create his own red-headed Venus, and Gwendolyn was the most perfect example of one whom he had ever seen. He considered if she refused, he would paint her face above the body of Luisa. But that seemed not quite right, not even to him. Luisa would probably not approve, anyway. He would just have to wait and see.

The week went by with Gwendolyn making progress on her own Venus. She did not give Rui's strange request a second thought. On Friday evening, with their after-dinner port wine, Rui was quite talkative about all manner of subjects. She just listened while admiring Botticelli's wonderful masterpiece, wondering what Rui was going on about.

Rui stopped, out of breath. He took another sip of port and was silent. He waited for her reaction. There was none coming. Many minutes and sips of port later, he finally screwed up his courage and said, "Well, Gwendolyn? Today's the end of the week. Will you please be my model? I would be most grateful."

Gwendolyn did not immediately answer. She knew this was causing him some stress, but she simply had not thought about it, hoping it might go away on its own.

"Look, Rui. The truth is I haven't thought about your… proposition all week. I'll give it some serious thought tonight and I'll let you know tomorrow. It really is a strange request. I still don't know what to make of it."

Realizing that she still had not refused him outright brought hope. He finished the bottle of port in twenty minutes and struggled to rise. "Well then, my dear, until tomorrow."

Luisa quickly appeared and helped her doddering man up to bed. Wheezing, he had to stop halfway up the stairs to rest. Luisa gently remonstrated with him in a loving, patient voice.

Meanwhile, Gwendolyn whispered to herself, *Rui, you are so lucky to have such an angel caring for you. I hope for your sake that you don't screw it up.*

Her thoughts drifted until they coalesced around his odd request. On the one hand, she did not think it was a good idea to be a nude model with a man whom she knew and was indeed living in his house with his dutiful but jealous mate. She needed nothing so complicated that it could explode, destroying the project even as it was coming closer to being finished.

On the other hand, Rui was completely harmless. If he had trouble walking up one flight of stairs, he would be useless in bed, especially trying to force himself on an unwilling woman. And she would always be an unwilling woman with him. Luisa seemed like a kindred spirit. She was wise enough to know when her very eccentric artist mate was crossing the line, though she was indulgent enough to blur the line at times.

After all, they were both artists, as Rui said. They were expected to be out of the norm. Posing as a model for a painting, nude or not, was simply how such things were done. She could not count how many times she painted nude men and women. They were not much different from painting a vase of flowers.

She decided she would do it as long as Rui could be absolutely certain that Luisa would not be a problem. Better yet, she would pose with Luisa in the studio. That should cover it. She would rise early and accompany Rui as he walked the dogs. She would tell him then. With that weight lifted, she rose and went to bed.

CHAPTER TEN

The next morning, as was his custom, Rui gathered up his dogs to leash them for their walk. They knew the drill. As soon as he opened the front door, they pulled him towards the gate, eager for their morning constitutional. Both dogs and man were surprised to meet Gwendolyn sitting on the stone bench by the statues of nude nymphs.

"Good morning, Rui. You don't mind if I join you today, would you?"

"Well, of course not. You're always welcome."

They followed the typical route that she remembered from when she secretly trailed him on that first day, which seemed years ago. They strolled up the hill chatting about unimportant things like how they slept and the weather. Rui clearly had his mind set on what her answer to his request would be.

As they turned to descend to the sea, she obliged him. "OK, Rui, here's my answer. I don't mind posing for your painting. The good Lord knows I've done that a hundred times in my younger days. However, this time it's not so simple. I am staying in your home for I don't know how long. And it so happens that living in the same home is a woman who has a jealous mind and is insecure about me being there."

"You mean Luisa? Oh, don't worry about her. She won't be a problem."

"Oh, yes, she would be a problem, Rui. In this regard, I know her better than you. Her having a strong reaction against it would be the most natural thing in the world. Not being bothered by it would be very strange, unnatural in fact. Unless, of course, she really doesn't care about you. We both know that's not true."

"OK, OK, if it makes you feel better, we'll do it when she's out doing errands. She's usually gone for a few hours when she does them."

"No, that's not a good idea. If she were to return sooner than expected and find us, oh, I'd hate to be there if that happens. Let me put it this way. If you would simply tell her that I will pose nude for your painting, what do you think she would say? How would she respond to the very idea of it?"

He paused and considered his proposal from a different angle. "Hmm, I see what you mean. She would not agree. Even asking her would produce a reaction that would take her a long time to calm down, maybe weeks, or probably longer. She might demand that you leave. Besides, it took me about three weeks to work up the courage to ask you in the first place."

"So, then, perhaps you should just drop the idea."

"No, I can't do that. I've been thinking of nothing else for weeks. I simply must paint you. It would be worth it to me even if she does leave me! There are thousands of middle-aged women who would love to take her place!" Rui's voice rose to a shout. Even the dogs whimpered at their distressed master.

"Calm down, Rui! The entire neighborhood can hear you. You're making your dogs upset, too."

Rui sped up, muttering to himself, "I simply must paint you. I must."

She realized he was clearly obsessed with painting her as he was obsessed with Botticelli's Venus above his fireplace. She never thought the normally calm and collected Rui would have this side to him. Yet the paintings in his studio undoubtedly indicated an obsession. What was it about this painting that caused grown men to lose their minds? Luckily, she had a solution.

"Wow, Rui, you really are obsessed about it. There may be thousands of middle-aged women out there, but there definitely are not thousands of Luisa's out there who would take care of you the way she does.

"Look, I'll tell you what I'm willing to do, for both our sakes. I'll pose for you only and only if she is in the studio with us. She can witness for herself the purely professional way that models and painters interact. I'll do it just this once for an afternoon, either today or tomorrow. If you need more time, you'll have to take a photo."

"Luisa in the studio? With us? Hm, I wonder how she would react to that. You're right, of course. That would be the best way. But how can I possibly bring up the subject… OK, I know. You present the idea to her. That might work. Would you?"

"Fine, I'll do that. I'll ask her after we're finished eating this morning. We'll see what she says."

"That's right. She'll either agree or not. If she doesn't, then we'll have to come up with a Plan B."

"Rui, there is no plan B. You'll need to wrap your head around that fact."

"Wrap my head around? I doubt I can do that if that sentence means what I think it means. Enough on this subject. Let's wait to hear her answer."

They finished the walk in silence. When they returned, brunch was on the sunroom table. As usual, every detail was lovingly addressed. Luisa was cheerful and chatty. Rui could respond only with grunts and single words. Gwendolyn had to rise to the occasion and keep Luisa in her high spirits. Her request would go much better if Luisa happened to be in an excellent mood.

After the last cup of coffee was finished, Luisa rose to clear the table. Gwendolyn also rose to help her. Rui did not stop her as he usually did. He gave her a furtive smile as she followed Luisa with cups and plates. Despite Luisa refusing her help, Gwendolyn insisted, with her arms laden with dishes.

"Gwendolyn, what are you doing?"

"I'm helping you clear the table."

"Well, don't. You're our guest and I'll not have guests help me with these things."

"Fine, but we're almost halfway to the kitchen. Do you want me to put these back on the table? Really?"

"OK, but only this once."

In the kitchen, they placed everything in and around the sink. Luisa turned to make her second trip. Gwendolyn blocked her path.

"Luisa, I need to ask you something." She paused.

"What is it, dear girl?"

"Rui wants me to pose for a painting."

"Rui wants you to pose for one of his paintings? Well, I guess I see nothing wrong with that. Why didn't he simply tell me?"

"That's just the thing. He thinks it would be better if I asked you. You see, he wants me to pose nude for his version of the Birth of Venus."

"You? Nude? The Birth of Venus? In his studio?" Luisa repeated with disbelief.

"Yes, yes, I know how ridiculous it sounds. I thought the same when he first asked me." Gwendolyn headed off her rising panic with the old tactic of agreeing on how preposterous a proposal sounds. "You understand that he wouldn't be painting me, but rather his idealized Venus. My form and figure would be merely that of his Venus, not mine. Heaven knows I'm no Venus. I haven't been spreading much physical love around lately.

"But listen. This is how I answered him. I told him I would only do it on one condition. And that is if you're with us in the studio while I posed."

This quieted Luisa. After a while, she replied, "Well, I know when you were students, you artists posed for other artists all the time, … nude or otherwise. And it was your idea for me to be present during this? Hm, I see. Well that certainly puts this in a wholly different light. Oh, aren't you so sweet for thinking of me and how I might feel about it."

She went silent and Gwendolyn judged it best not to interrupt her. Finally, she broke the silence. "And when does he want to do this?"

"Either this afternoon or tomorrow. I also told him I would only do it once."

Again, some silence passed. "You would only agree if I was there? To watch you pose for him nude? Really?"

Gwendolyn nodded.

"You artists are really too much… Fine, let's do it today. In the nude? Really? Wow! I must say I didn't see that coming. I tell you. Rui and this crazy obsession with his Venus." She squeezed Gwendolyn's shoulder and looked deeply into her eyes. "After thinking about it, I wouldn't mind if you pose for him for as long as you like. Days, weeks, whatever it takes."

Gwendolyn was at a loss for words. Her somewhat shocked face made Luisa realize she was being too enthusiastic about it and quickly added, "What I'm trying to say is, don't be nervous about doing it on my account. I'm not as prudish an old fuddy-duddy as I may look. I still have a sense of adventure." She smiled as she stepped past her to bring back more plates. "I'll deal with the rest. You can put crazy Rui's mind at ease."

Gwendolyn followed her back to the table and returned to her place next to Rui. After Luisa left with another load of dishes, she gave him a thumbs up. His face immediately beamed with joy. "She agreed to do it this afternoon. Let's plan around 1300. Would that be fine?"

"Why not now? OK, OK 1300 it is. Meet me in the studio on time with Luisa." He rose to do various things in his office, though he could not concentrate on anything else. At last, he could create his own Venus, his own beautiful redheaded Goddess of Love.

As for the living breathing redheaded Venus, she retired to the garden to continue reading The Book of Disquiet. Soon, Luisa joined her with her book of poetry. At the appointed time, Rui hurried past them to his studio. "Shall we, ladies? It's already 1300."

Gwendolyn sighed, "Ok, let's get this over with." They followed him into the studio. He had already set up on the easel the large, prepped canvas that was the same size as the one in the living room. Its base coat was already dry and ready for painting the figures. He had already laid out the paint and brushes in anticipation that the planets might align, and Gwendolyn would agree. No time to waste.

"OK, Gwendolyn, we have only about five hours of good sunlight. Stand there where the sun will shine on you at a side angle. You can hang your clothes on those wooden pegs on the wall over there."

She put her book down on a side table and walked over to the wooden pegs to undress. Luisa followed her over. "Sweety, let me undress you."

"Luisa, I know we're kindred spirits and all that, but I can undress myself. Thanks for your kind offer, though." She thought to herself, *What an odd couple they are. They make the Robinsons seem perfectly normal.* As she undressed, she recalled the forgery project immediately before the current one, when that LA couple was killed in their home by Russian agents of Popov, and they pinned the murder on her. She almost failed at trying to find the real culprits. (read The Eye of the Beholder). *I hope nothing happens to these kind but eccentric people.*

After taking her appointed position, Gwendolyn discreetly covered herself like Botticelli's famous Venus in the Uffizi Museum. Both Rui and Luisa took a moment to admire the physical beauty of their house guest in all her glory. Luisa admired how nicely shaved she was. She could not keep her eyes off her guest's nether region. Rui murmured to himself, "If I was twenty years younger, you wouldn't have a chance, sweet thing."

More loudly, he said, "That's fine, but Gwendolyn, I want you to pose like my Venus above the fireplace. Look directly at me with lust and desire in your eyes with your hands placed like hers just above your quim."

"Like this?"

"Yes, except place your fingers further down, on your maiden hair. Nicely trimmed, by the way. You know, like how she does it in my painting."

She rolled her eyes, but followed his instructions, already regretting she agreed to do this ridiculous thing. He continued, "Exactly so. As you suggested, I will take a photo of you so I can continue after today, unless you've changed your mind about only doing this once."

"Just this once, Rui. Shall we get on with it?"

Rui pulled out an old Polaroid camera from a drawer and took her picture. He pinned the just-printed photo on the wall by his easel.

"Yes, yes. Let's do." Rui spent the remaining part of the afternoon busily laying the foundation of his Birth of Venus. He gave her a five-minute break once an hour. Normally, the models would take a cigarette break. Gwendolyn did not smoke, but she welcomed the opportunity to sit down and rest a bit. There was only one place to sit, a chair covered with a towel beside Luisa. She took her breaks completely nude. It made no sense to cover herself.

Luisa was positively enthusiastic, delighted in fact by the whole thing. "What a beautifully taut and tight body you have, sweet Gwendolyn, full of the bloom and blush of youth. How I envy you!"

"Come now, Luisa, I'm sure you had your time of youthful beauty. I bet you still have plenty of your own, even now." She immediately regretted responding so politely.

"Are you serious? Do you honestly think so? Maybe we can compare our bodies sometime?"

Gwendolyn realized she needed Rui there as a chaperone as much as she needed Luisa. "Compare? What for? Our faces can reveal all that is necessary, don't you agree? Our bodies are mere physical husks holding our true natures. She leaned back with her eyes closed, *Please, dear Earth! Please turn faster away from the sun!*

By the end of the day, in the sun's fading light, Rui had managed to capture her figure with its various curves and forms. He also captured her flowing red hair, though he would have to make it longer for the painting. He did not waste time filling in the details of her face. Her face would be available to him whenever he looked at her. He could include all the remaining specifics and figures later by using his memory without her being present. He intended to paint himself as Zephyr and Luisa as Chloris. As for Flora? He would have to think about that.

"Come here, please. Take a look at what I've done so far. What do you think?"

"Give me a minute. Let me dress myself first."

She did so and approached Rui's easel. She had to admit to herself that, despite the amateur that he was, he did an excellent job reproducing the forms and colors of the painting above his fireplace.

"I must say, Rui, you've done remarkable work. I can definitely recognize my body and face there. And my hair. You have the color exactly right. Good for you."

She could not help but notice the irony of them both recreating Botticelli's strange version that somehow found itself hanging in the living room of this peculiar couple. She supposed that if Giles simply stole the Botticelli and did not wait for her reproduction, that Rui would willingly replace it with his own version. He would lean back in his high-backed stuffed leather chair, admiring her, either Venus, or Gwendolyn, or even both of them merged together while he drank his after-dinner port wine and not dwell too much on it.

"I'm so pleased you agree. And Gwendolyn, thank you so very much for this. You have no idea how much this means to me."

She stopped herself from mechanically saying 'anytime' and instead replied, "Hey, no problem. Glad I could help. Now, if you don't mind, I think I'll go shower and rest. Holding a pose for so long is very tiring." Exhausted, she left the studio.

She locked her door and indulged in a long bath, hoping to wash off the lustful glances she had to endure all afternoon. She admitted she was very surprised at Luisa's reaction. Objectively, it certainly helped her position there if they both wanted her to stay. But not like this. Posing for Rui's fantasy Venus took an unexpectedly odd turn. She closed her eyes to consider her new situation from every angle.

Luisa obviously had a different interest in her than before. But how serious was she, really? Would Gwendolyn have to fend her off? What if it came to that? Would Luisa become furious at being spurned? How would Rui take it? Then the whole situation would be reversed. Would he become jealous and throw her out? Or would he become very interested and want to watch them? She shuddered at the thought.

She still had to get through dinner and her normal evening conversation with Rui. A deep sigh of aggravation and frustration escaped her lips. She closed her tired eyes and lowered her body under the hot bath water until just her nose stuck out.

CHAPTER ELEVEN

By Monday morning, Gwendolyn's daily routine was back on track. First, brunch at 0900, then painting her Birth of Venus for seven or eight hours in her bungalow studio. At the end of the day, she would detour to the beach and watch the sun set over Cascais Harbor, filled with bare bobbing masts serenely casting their bony shadows on the darkening water. Later, she would return to Rui's home with the dying light to guide her and have a wonderful dinner at 2000, followed by artistic conversation before the master's Venus.

Three weeks passed. One morning at brunch Rui hesitated before he announced that he and his friends would have one of their periodic ritual celebrations of Venus in two weeks. Luisa immediately showed her anger, "Oh, Rui! Really? When will you grow up? Don't tell me that loathsome George will be here under our roof?"

"Now, dearest, we have discussed this many times before. I only do this a few times a year. And yes, of course, he'll be here for it. He leads it. He requested that I organize it with our usual group. As always, everyone will be gone before morning."

She suddenly slammed her knife and fork down on the table before storming off. Rui turned to the perturbed Gwendolyn, "Don't worry, my dear. She always gets upset when I tell her I'm doing this. She'll be fine in a few days."

"She'll be fine in a few days? What exactly will you be doing that causes her to react like that?"

"Oh, it's nothing really. Just a bunch of absurd middle-aged men having a silly boozy party."

"If it's so silly, why do it at all if she hates it so much?"

"Let's just say it's complicated. It means a lot to George. It's the only thing I indulge him with. Besides, he's a far older friend than Luisa. He is very important to me. Still. You just stay in your room out of his sight and go to sleep, as usual. There's nothing for you to worry about."

After he remained silent for a few minutes, staring out at the garden, she excused herself and walked the short distance to her studio bungalow to continue her painting. That George would be there even for a few hours made her uneasy. She would simply hide in her locked room and stay out of sight as instructed. With that, she ignored it and concentrated on the task at hand.

That evening's sunset was particularly beautiful, with its red-tinged golden glow blanketing the waters with its warm reflection. Despite the dazzling light show displayed before her, her thoughts returned to her modeling Venus for Rui a few weeks before. In hindsight, she regretted that she had let him talk her into it.

Ordinarily, she would think nothing of posing as a model for a fellow painter. But there seemed to be more to it than just another work of art. Considering his other odd paintings scattered throughout his studio, she sensed something perverted about it. Luisa's vehement reaction against his Venus stag party only increased her misgivings.

How she wished she could finish her painting and get out of there before yet another unpleasant thing happened. She knew she could not rush. Between the oil paint needing time to dry and every detail requiring painstaking care, she had no choice but to see it to its conclusion. Giles had told her often that she could walk away anytime if she ever felt uncomfortable. She reassured herself that there was nothing that she could not manage.

As the day of the Venus ritual neared, Gwendolyn became more fascinated by it. A few days before the strange evening would arrive, she found Luisa sitting in the garden sun, reading her poetry. As he had predicted, she was much calmer. Gwendolyn approached her and sat by her in the shade.

"Hello, Luisa. What are you reading today?"

"Oh, hi. Glad you can join me. I'm reading Jorge de Sena's Perseguição. He was a surrealist poet from the 1940s. Have you heard of him?"

"No, I can't say I have. What I want to ask you is about Rui's Venus party coming up soon. Why did you have such a strong reaction when he announced it? What goes on during these parties?"

"Oh, Gwendolyn, don't worry yourself over it. It's the only sticking point between Rui and me. I just wish he would stop doing them. But somehow, he simply cannot refuse that bastard George who puts far more importance to these things than he does. I hate George. There's something evil about him. I cringe at the thought that his shadow will darken our home."

"I get that. I felt creepy when I saw him for that short time I did. But what do they do during these parties that cause such a reaction in you?"

"You really don't want to know. You'll think less of him. I certainly do."

"But what do they do? Do they sacrifice a lamb? Do they have a great big gay orgy? Please, I'm genuinely intrigued."

Luisa burst into laughter. "No, silly girl. They don't do anything that interesting. It's a lot of drinking and doing foolish, fake, ritualistic things. For example, they bring in several prostitutes and have them wear red hair wigs, pretending to be the Venus of the painting. That's mostly it."

"Well, what do they do with the women? Sacrifice them?"

"No, no sacrifices, nothing that serious. Besides, it would take too much effort."

"OK, then what do they do with the prostitutes?"

"What do you think? As for Rui, he only sits in the corner and watches the crazy spectacle with his bottle of port wine close at hand. At least he has enough respect for me to do nothing more."

"What about George? What does he do?"

"He prances about like a witch doctor or a shaman conducting the whole thing."

"How do you know all this? Have you seen it?"

"Yes, I peeked through the window the first time. Nothing's changed about it after all these years. Look, I don't want to discuss it anymore. I have only just calmed down and talking about it's getting me worked up again. As for you, you must not show your face to anyone, especially George. Remove it completely from your mind. Do you understand?"

"Yes, Luisa, I believe I do."

"Fine. I'll see you for dinner." She opened her book and turned away.

Gwendolyn caught her meaning and left to resume her painting. Nonetheless, throughout the rest of that day and the few remaining days until the Saturday night of the bizarre ritual led by their warped witch doctor, nothing else consumed her thoughts. Her curiosity would not give her mind any peace.

Finally, the big day came. Gwendolyn took Luisa's advice and dismissed the outlandish pagan rites to Venus from her thoughts by concentrating on her painting. It was quite a productive day. She returned to the house with a calm mind, pleased with how her work was progressing. In only a few more weeks she could escape the strange couple.

It was a quiet dinner. Rui barely ate a thing, toying with his food. Gwendolyn thought he would be excited about the upcoming special event. "Rui, why aren't you eating? Is something bothering you?"

Rui acted as if he did not hear her. Luisa answered, "Because George told him he is not supposed to eat anything during the day before the rites. Isn't that right, Rui?"

He nodded. She continued, "Yet, you ate a big brunch and an afternoon snack. Only now you remember what the crazy circus master told you."

Rui ignored her. "Gwendolyn, now listen carefully. George and the other guests will arrive in a little over an hour. I would like you to go to your room and lock the door. Luisa will sit outside to prevent any unwanted attention being directed to the locked attic. Keep the windows and the curtains shut. Only use the small reading lamp by your bed. Ignore anything strange you might hear. I'll see you tomorrow for brunch at the normal time. Is that OK?"

"OK, Rui, I guess. Now you're making this thing sound even more mysterious. I thought it was just a ridiculous drinking party admiring Botticelli's wonderful painting."

"Some people take it far more seriously, but, yes, that's what it is, basically. Don't pay it any mind. We're already giving it more significance than it deserves by even talking about it. Now, if you'll excuse me, I need to get things ready."

With that, dinner was over. Luisa accompanied Gwendolyn to her room. At the top of the stairs, Luisa lowered her voice. "The only reason we're taking these precautions is because of George. If he knew Rui had a redhead staying with us in the same house as his revered Venus, he might flip into the deep end. None of the other infantile old men would care. In fact, they might find it all fascinating and pursue you like depraved fauns in an ancient Greek forest filled with the music of Debussy. Don't worry. I'll not let evil George or anyone else bother you tonight. If you need anything, I'll be right outside your door. Now good night."

Gwendolyn thanked her for everything, closed the door, and locked it. She read a little, then turned off the small lamp. She stared at the dark ceiling for a while before turning over to sleep. But sleep eluded her. She heard Luisa snoring through the door, as she sat sleeping at the top of the stairs, leaning against the locked door. That did not help Gwednolyn's futile attempts to sleep.

Curiosity reared its dark, puzzling head in her mind. What would happen at this ritual? As she forced those thoughts out, she heard the front door open and groups of already tipsy men making boisterous sounds as they entered. She could not make out the meaning. Things quieted down as they moved into the living room. Soon after, several young women entered with their intoxicated high voices shrieking with laughter. Silence followed as they entered after the men.

She tried to ignore it all and go to sleep as she was told. She gave up after two hours of tossing and turning while her mind imagined all sorts of fantastic ritualistic dancing and orgies like in a Hieronymus Bosch painting. It was after midnight, the witching hour. She could take it no more. Dressed for the chilly night air, she quietly opened the window and climbed through to the terrace open to the stars.

A heavy metal drainpipe attached to the edge carried rainwater from the roof to the ground. She grabbed hold and slid down, landing softly on the grass. Sticking to the shadows, she carefully snuck to the window of the living room, which offered a view of the entire affair. She stood a few steps back from the window so she could peer in without them seeing her. The scene in front of her seemed like a prehistoric cave ritual, with painted images of the recent hunt on rock walls, surrounded by superstitious men celebrating the animal spirits' generosity.

The difference was, instead of paintings of prehistoric horses, bison, and mammoths, animals long extinct, the focus of these wild cavemen was a Renaissance painting of a young lusty nude woman standing on a huge scallop shell floating on the ocean. The room was almost empty of furniture. The lights were turned off. Large candles gave the only illumination, resting on tall carved wooden stands against the walls.

The fire roaring in the fireplace cast long shadows against the opposite wall. A wide table at the back was full of bottles, jars of white powder, and yellowed Meerschaum pipes propped up on wooden mounts with wisps of smoke slowly rising to disappear in the darkness above.

Nearly thirty soft and flabby nude men all well past fifty, wildly danced. Each wore animal masks. There were bears with their very hairy backs lumbering about with paws in the air. Old flabby bulls pranced on all fours. There were tigers, horses, wolves, even a very hirsute mammoth with a fully erect trunk. Each gesticulated and gyrated as his pretended nature required. They grunted, bellowed, or growled according to their animal spirits.

Below the painting, the five prostitutes, standing nude on pedestals arrayed before the fireplace, were shimmying lewdly. Venus would have been proud of them. Each of them had masks, too, but they were masks of Botticelli's wanton Venus. Barely visible in the far corner on the only chair in the room sat a nude Rui. He was the only one without a mask or other animal adornment and appeared to be merely a spectator.

Leaping and dancing around the entire group, the shaman conducted the wild ritual. It was George, the only one without a mask. Instead he had attached a pair of great antlers tightly to his head. He was nude as well, except for a codpiece identical to a falcon's face with its protruding sharp beak, like the figure in the Dutch Renaissance painter Frans Floris' The Fall of the Rebel Angels. He had painted his face and body to look like a voodoo skeleton. In one hand, he held a black knife that glinted in the firelight. In the other, he appeared to hold a thigh bone. Was it human? It was the size of one.

Suddenly he shrieked and everyone stopped their animal movements and sounds. The prostitutes slipped down from their pedestals, while the men gathered before them on their knees and chanted with an urgent voice of supplication. The conducting shaman let out another high-pitched screech, and the women, turning toward the fireplace, assumed the position. The crazed animal men mated with each of them with a wild bestial abandon, such that their wives at home had probably never experienced. While most eagerly waited for their turn, several others, too impatient to wait, paired up with their fellow celebrants at the darker edges away from the main group.

Animal sounds again filled the room, rising to a pitch with each successful mating. The five Venus pretenders screamed with delight. Rui did not stir from his seat. Several times, George tried to entice him to slip back into old habits, but Rui gently pushed him away each time.

Without noticing, Gwendolyn had slowly approached closer to see the spectacle better. After witnessing the bizarre scene for an hour, she was right next to the window. George looked at the window and thought he saw a redheaded spy peering in. He stopped and stared. She quickly pulled away. He had already caught sight of her and immediately screamed violently, stopping everything in mid-stroke.

"A demon! A demon is spying on us. Quick! We must catch the foul piece of excrement and destroy her before she can report back to her masters. Follow me!"

He directed one group of nude animal spirits to circle around one side of the house while he took the rest around the other side. Rui followed him to intervene, if necessary, already guessing what caused the extreme agitation in George. They met behind the house with no demon found. George ordered them to beat the garden shrubs and bushes for any creeping demon. The bush beaters found nothing to flush out. Gwendolyn had already disappeared up the rainwater pipe, shut the window, threw her clothes into the bathroom, and leapt into bed.

George was furious. "Rui! Are you keeping a red demon in your house? Tell me!"

Rui was equally livid. "The only demon in this house is you. Get control of yourself. Everyone! Stop damaging my garden! Let's all go back inside. There is still unfinished business."

Those who had been patiently waiting for their time to partake of the fruits of Venus agreed and returned to the waiting women. The cool of the night encouraged the others to follow.

Only George remained with Rui, eyeing him. George looked up at the attic window. The edge of the curtain fluttered in the night breeze where the window had closed on it. "She's up there, isn't she?" He suddenly ran inside and up the stairs towards the attic. Rui grabbed him by the shoulders and threw him onto the floor. The commotion had woken Luisa.

"George! Are you crazy? Control yourself!" George stopped struggling and calmly sat up.

"Rui. I'll ask you just once. Do you have a young redheaded woman staying with you in the attic room?"

"You're completely insane! You're imagining things. You saw nothing because there's nothing to see. This is my home. Show some respect!"

"Answer me!"

Luisa was livid. "Rui, remove this stain from our home and never let it back in again. If you don't, I'll grab him and throw him out myself, but only after I beat him to a pulp." She grabbed a heavy candlestick holder and threw the snuffed-out candle on the floor.

"George, you must leave now. Not another word. Leave! Now!"

Rui pulled him up with one arm around his neck and the other grabbing his shoulder. He manhandled George down the stairs. Luisa opened the front door.

"OK, OK, Rui. I'm leaving. Will you at least let me put my clothes on?"

"Fine. But be quick about it."

George found his clothes among the piles of discarded vestments in the foyer. He dressed and walked out the open front door. As he passed Rui, "OK, friend, I'm leaving. You are too important for me to lose you. But I promise you I'll find her. Oh, I will find her."

"Get out!" Rui pushed him out of the front gate and slammed it shut after him.

Luisa whispered hoarsely, "Rui, it's time to end this grotesque charade. And put your clothes on, for heaven's sake."

"I agree."

Gwendolyn lay shaking under the blankets. She heard the raving George just outside her door. She was thankful for them protecting her, but realized she had caused a major conflict between them by doing exactly what she was told not to do. Her questions were definitively answered, but at what price? How could she face her two hosts at brunch the next morning? She should probably pack her bags and prepare an explanation for Giles as to why their project failed. Normally the very epitome of professionalism, her face reddened with shame. Oh, how she would hate to let him down! Why did she not control her stupid curiosity?

Sleep was impossible for the rest of the night.

CHAPTER TWELVE

Only Luisa showed up for brunch the following morning. Rui slept in late to recover from all the craziness of the night before. Gwendolyn was extremely worried that he would be angry with her and rightly so, considering her acting on her dangerous curiosity put everything in jeopardy, maybe even her life. Who knows what George would have done if he had caught her?

Gwendolyn did not dare look at Luisa. She picked at her food. Finally, testing the waters, she asked, "How's Rui?"

"Oh, he's fine. He always needs to recover from those stupid rituals, or 'parties' as he calls them, though he does nothing but drink too much."

"Luisa, I heard the conflict with George outside my door last night. I really must say that I'm so…"

"Listen, Gwendolyn, I don't care what you did or didn't do last night to get him to lose it like he did. But I thank you anyway. Rui is at last realizing just how bad that old false friend of his is. I hope he can finally close that sordid chapter of his life and move on. George is not only a horrible person, but also a negative influence on him. So enough said on the subject. Would you care for some smoked salmon with your eggs?"

With that, Gwendolyn relaxed and ate her food. They talked about literature and poetry, having a good time without Rui being present. He would only talk about art. She wished to get back to her painting and so took her leave, only somewhat later than normal.

As she shut the gate, Gwendolyn felt she needed the ocean breeze to calm her nervous heart. She walked directly down the hill to the beach instead of turning right at the corner to go to her bungalow.

She passed a thuggish-looking man on the corner with a dog on a leash. He grunted as she walked past him, causing her to look at his face. His eyes could not conceal his loathing of her. He roughly yanked the dog closer to him. The dog yelped in complaint.

The strange encounter unsettled her. As Gwendolyn continued, she considered how she had never seen the man walking his dog at the hour she normally went to her studio. Usually, walking one's dog was a routine that never changed. The way he looked at her indicated he knew her or of her somehow. She had walked a block when it struck her. He must be one of George's men tasked with following her. She stopped and turned around. He was following her, just half a block away. He stopped, too, pretending to study flowers growing near the sidewalk.

She turned and strode quickly to her ocean destination, causing him to pick up his pace as well. *Oh George, you pathetic excuse. You really need to find henchmen who understand how to tail someone.*

Gwendolyn entered the tunnel under the Estoril train station that led to the beach. She spun around and ran up the stairway to the station. But instead of continuing forward, she doubled back and hid in the entrance to the boarded-up restaurant facing the Avenida Marginal, the busy coastal roadway between Lisboa and Cascais. She saw him hurry up the stairs after her and towards the station, tugging the poor, complaining dog after him. Smiling at how easy that was, she pressed on in the opposite direction to the next intersection, where she could cross over and continue to her bungalow studio.

Passing the main entrance to the hotel, she proceeded to the next corner. Scanning the streets in all four directions, she sighed with relief that no one else followed her. She turned left and continued further up to the old modest metal door that was the hotel's back entrance for the long-term residents of the bungalows.

With the sound of the door locking behind her, she sank down on her bungalow bed. She smiled at the ease of losing the goon, but soon her smile slowly disappeared. She was safe for the moment, but now George was sure she was staying at Rui's. He could send someone to tail her every day, trying to learn her daily habits. Perhaps looking for the perfect time and place to grab her and do the gods know what with her. George, in his murderous rage the night before, clearly was not interested in giving her a lecture on etiquette.

Gwendolyn thought of calling Giles, but then reconsidered it. He would only demand she immediately stop everything. She was on the verge of completing her masterpiece, just a few weeks more. She rose to start on her painting, but then soon realized she was in no condition to do anything serious at the moment. She returned to her bed and collapsed, promptly falling into a deep dreamless sleep. The events of the previous night and the morning were proving too much. She needed a nap.

About two hours later, she awoke, feeling significantly better. She arose and restarted her earlier attempt at painting. Her mind was clear and rested. She made substantial progress on the giant scallop shell that was lifting Venus from the watery depths.

Later, at dinner, Rui was quite chirpy and cheerful, clearly glad to see Gwendolyn. He asked his guest who she thought was her favorite famous Portuguese painter.

"Not sure about my favorite painter, but I can say without hesitation who my least favorite is."

"And who may that be?"

"Paula Rego."

Rui laughed. "Paula Rego. Oh, really? Why her?"

"I know she's considered a quasi-goddess here. I genuinely admire the architecture of her museum here in Cascais. Looks like something one might find in Timbuktu. It's not her technique that I have any problem with. It's her style and subject matter. Everything and everyone is ugly. She clearly had issues with men, considering how she treats them in her paintings, usually as devilish infants.

"Most of her subjects were women, all obviously insane. Probably reflecting her own mental health. She clearly needed to be stretched out on a psychiatric couch. Maybe medication and professional care could have helped her, but then she would not have achieved such fame and success if she had not been psychologically disturbed. Much of her art revolved around abortion. I think the Portuguese adore her only because she is famous in foreign countries and not for any artistic greatness."

"Whoa, Gwendolyn, that's quite an indictment of our people. There must be a reason why the London elite values her so greatly. Personally, I have to say I don't completely disagree with you. I visited one of her shows in London when I was living there. We met. You should have seen how they fawned all over her, treating her like a celebrity, which I guess she was.

"Despite us being both Portuguese, she spoke English with me the entire conversation. As you can tell, I have no problem speaking the Queen's English. Nonetheless, I thought she was being rather pretentious. I was young and in my prime. She abruptly stopped what we were talking about and asked me if I would like to follow her into the back room of the gallery to show me something special. I was not so naive as to fail to understand what she meant.

"Luckily, or unluckily, I still can't decide, I turned down her kind offer in the politest way I knew how. In those days I was not interested in what she had to give anyway. She was about ten years older than me. I must admit she was rather attractive in her cinnamon-colored Portuguese sort of way. George accompanied me to the show and spent most of the event standing in front of one of her paintings, spying on me with sidelong glances. I wonder what he would have done if I had followed her swaying hips to the back. Probably he would have made some sort of scene. Well, it's all quite moot now.

"It was clear then that she had, as we would say today, issues. Perhaps medication and psychiatrists would have helped, but they also would have most likely buried her artistic impulses. But yes, we Portuguese appreciate any accolades we can get from whomever and whatever source, especially from foreigners."

Luisa was pleased to see him being so warm and caring with Gwendolyn. It's possible she might help in the long and drawn-out process of weaning him from George's evil influence. She was confident that nothing would ever transpire between the two. Rui truly treated her more like the daughter he never had.

The next morning, Gwendolyn set out for her studio as usual. Also, as she feared, she was followed by another ugly thuggish man walking a dog. She led him to the Estoril Casino. Security guards stopped him from entering because of the dog. He let the dog run free so he could follow her into the casino. The guards still would not allow him to enter, ordering him to retrieve his fleeing dog. He gave up and she continued on her way.

The next day, two others attempted to tail her. She lost them in the Casino, anyway. The day after that, a car followed her. She led them down one of the many one-way streets and then reversed direction so it could not turn around and follow her. Another time, the same car attempted to pursue her. Before she could trap them again in a one-way street, a pair of ruffians leapt out. They tried to seize her and pull her into the car. She dodged them and ran away, screaming to alert anyone in the area of her plight. They quickly drove away.

That experience made her decide to call a taxi the next day to take her pursuers on a wild goose chase. They followed the taxi closely, not even trying to be secretive. Gwendolyn told the driver to stop at the bottom of another one-way street. She paid him extra to stay there, blocking the road for a minute so she could disappear out of sight.

It turned into a game for her. She enjoyed outsmarting the goons. Every day she did so, she was closer to finishing the painting. She knew it was a dangerous game, to be sure. Since they did not simply shoot her dead in a drive-by killing as they do in Los Angeles must have meant that George wanted her alive. She wondered in trepidation what exactly that meant.

On the following day, no one followed her. She was relieved except for the little shadow that was always near her. She looked up at the source of a quiet but steady hum. A drone hovered above her. Because canopies of trees covered most streets, she could easily lose it, too.

In the middle of the day, Gwendolyn visited a nearby dusty wooden toy shop, named Happy Woodland (Bosque Feliz). Everything was hand carved wood with nothing made in China in the entire place. She found what she hoped would be there: a child's slingshot. The store owner refurbished it with a powerful, new rubber band. He sold her a sack of marbles.

The following day, she allowed the drone to hover above her, getting a closer look. She quickly pulled out her new sling shot, loaded several marbles, aimed, and fired. She shot the drone out of the sky with sparks flying. Picking it up, she stared into the camera. Unleashing a string of expletives, she gave it the old Bronx salute, and then smashed the offending object into tiny pieces on the sidewalk.

The day after, no one and no thing followed her. A week passed without any threatening strangers tailing her. By the second week, Gwendolyn accepted that they gave up on her. This was a great relief. Another week went by. She had completed her masterpiece. It only required a few days to dry, and Giles could do the rest. She informed him of the good news. But Rui and Luisa needed to be out of the house for at least a few hours. How could she arrange that?

Three weeks passed and still Rui and Luisa showed no signs of leaving, not even to see a play or a jazz performance. Instead of going to her studio, Gwendolyn spent her days in the garden reading, growing more nervous with each passing day. For his part, Rui was becoming more hopeful that she had perhaps decided to stay and make his home hers.

One Monday at brunch, believing Gwendolyn had settled in for the long-term, Rui felt confident enough to announce that on the coming Friday he had to go up country to the northeast, where he had a large cork plantation in the Alto Alentejo. It was harvesting season for the cork trees, and he needed about a week or more to make sure everything ran smoothly.

He would fly there with Luisa and the dogs in his small plane. He invited Gwendolyn to go with them. Her heart leapt. This was her chance to switch the paintings! She graciously declined. After all, it would be great if Rui and Luisa had some time to be alone together. Luisa beamed at the thought. Rui wanted to press the issue, but Luisa came to the rescue by immediately agreeing that would be a fantastic idea.

That Wednesday, while taking a long walk for exercise, Gwendolyn checked on her painting. It was exactly as wonderful as she left it, a perfect copy of Rui's painting that was just impatiently waiting to have a change of view with a different owner in a new location. She called Giles and told him the good news. Rui, Luisa, and the dogs would all be gone for at least a week, starting from Friday morning. They could switch the paintings any time after that.

She assured him that she was fully packed and prepared to check out of the hotel that Friday evening. His team would meet her there late in the afternoon so they could frame then pack it for the quick trip to Rui's living room. Giles' congratulations on a job well done brought a warm glow of satisfaction to Gwendolyn's heart. Yes, she had finished an impressive work despite several complications.

CHAPTER THIRTEEN

The big day of the switch arrived. As usual, Gwendolyn met Rui and Luisa at brunch. The dogs were walked, and everything packed in the car for the brief trip to the Cascais airport. There was not much conversation. She yearned to fast forward to when she would meet Giles later that day at her soon-to-be abandoned studio. Rui was a little sad that he was soon to part from his favorite living artist and Venus model, even for a short time. Luisa was taciturn, as was her nature.

Luisa quickly cleaned up the remains of their meal while Rui took care of a few things in his office. Finally, the time of their departure came. Gwendolyn walked them to the gate. Rui suddenly turned and nervously asked her: "Are you sure you don't want to come with us? It'll be fun and interesting for you."

"Yes, definitely. You two have a great trip."

"You have all the keys, and the kitchen is well stocked. Help yourself to the wine. You know where I keep the port. We'll only be gone for a week, ten days at the most. Here is my calling card. It has this address and my cellphone number. If there's anything you need, anything at all, just call me, OK? I can be back here in an hour, two at the most."

"Thanks, Rui. I'm positive I'll be fine. I might finish the Book of Disquiet by the time you return."

"Ah, the Book of Disquiet in the house of quiet." He chuckled. "OK. We'll return before you know it."

Gwendolyn closed the creaking metal gate and waved as the old Range Rover disappeared down the road. She returned to her room and packed up her belongings. She left her painting of the yacht on the wall as a parting gift. For the remaining hours, she perched on a divan in the garden and read Fernando Pessoa's famous book. She ate a late lunch of the reheated omelet and the smoked salmon. She did not know when or even if she would have dinner that night. Giles usually forgot   about eating when working.

She was relaxed as she walked to her bungalow for the last time. She had seen none of George's idiot goons trying to follow her for several weeks already. They clearly gave up hassling her. She dodged that bullet. She pondered where to go for a break after it was all over, considering first one coastal town then another.

In her studio, she packed up everything. She sat on the veranda and finished the remaining bottle of wine, admiring her work. After all, her job was done. All that remained was Giles' responsibility. Her Venus was dry and ready for the short trip to her new home. She would be revered and adored just as much as her (greatly) older sister, who for her part would experience the same on a new wall by different admirers.

It was early evening when Giles arrived with his team of helpers. Dressed in workmen's clothes, they carried toolboxes and carefully wrapped wooden parts. They looked like any other group of renovators. He never considered what people might think of renovators arriving at a hotel room at such an hour. Luckily, no one even noticed. As they framed the painting, he sat beside her.

"Sorry I'm late. We met with a few complications, but we're all past that now."

"No problem. We have plenty of time. Would you care for some wine?"

"You know I never drink when I'm working. I must say, you've really outdone yourself this time. This is truly an excellent work of art. Have you thought of where you would like to go for your well-deserved vacation?"

"Not yet. Thanks to your help in getting my French residency, I don't have any restrictions   for staying in Europe. Maybe I'll go down south to a secluded beach resort to decompress. I don't know, maybe the Algarve. Perhaps I might try somewhere on the Mediterranean coast like Amalfi or even Corfu. Hey, perhaps I'll go further south to Morocco. My mind's been too preoccupied with finishing my Venus. Let me sleep on it. I'll tell you tomorrow."

Meanwhile, Giles' team carefully prepared the painting and placed it in the period wooden frame, an exact replica of the one hanging above Rui's fireplace. Then they wrapped the painting in a protective covering. Finally, everything was ready. It was already after 2230 and our heavenly lunar neighbor was busily climbing the night sky.

They loaded the painting into a van marked Vidra de Vida, Lda. It had to be big enough to transport such a sizable painting. The only one Giles could find was a van for transporting large panes of glass. She checked out of the hotel and sat in the front seat to help navigate the narrow, one-way streets.

Presently, they arrived at the dark house. Gwendolyn opened the double gate for the van to back in. They followed her into the house and into the living room. Down came Rui's painting and quickly was wrapped for safe transport. Up went Gwendolyn's version and carefully installed in the space vacated. They put Botticelli's Venus in the back of the van. The entire operation took less than ten minutes.

Giles whispered, "OK, let's go."

"Giles, it's late. I think I'll spend one more night here. I'll meet you tomorrow at your hotel for brunch."

"Really? Why?"

"I kind of formed an attachment to this place and the odd doddering Rui. There's no rush. He won't be back for at least a week."

"But what about George? Aren't you worried what he might do?"

"Nah. I've seen no sign of them for several weeks. I just want to sit in front of my painting and drink some more of Rui's aged port one last time. I think I owe myself that. Don't worry. I'll be fine."

"Are you sure?"

"Yes, I'm sure. Now get going."

"OK. But I don't like it. I'll have one of the crew stay here with you, just in case. José is dependable and burly enough to defend the both of you."

"If he's not at least a delightful conversationalist, I'm not interested."

"He's an MFA from the University of Lisboa. He found my employment offer more attractive than what the current art market is offering. His specialty was the art of Paula Rego."

"Paula Rego? Oh, this should be an interesting conversation. I'll keep an open mind and see what flash of insight he can give me.

Fine, but he'll sleep in one of the guest bedrooms. My door will be locked for the night."

"You're quite the vain one. What makes you think he'd even be interested?"

"What? Even if he was batting for the other team, you don't think I could persuade him to join mine?"

"Batting for the other team? Now Gwendolyn, there's no reason to be crude about it. And, no, I don't doubt your ability to convince someone to switch teams, as you put it."

"Me being crude? What's crude about 'batting for the other team'? …Oh, no, I didn't mean 'batting' in any other meaning than a simple sport's metaphor. You have cricket and we have baseball. You're the crude one for thinking like that. Besides, you taught me that silly expression. Remember? Wow! This conversation really sank fast. Look, just send him in and be on your way. I'll see you tomorrow, say 1000. OK?"

"See you tomorrow at ten am on the dot." Giles chuckled to himself as he climbed into the driver's seat. He gave José a few quick instructions, who then exited the van and helped Gwendolyn close the gate behind the Glass of Life van. He followed her back inside.

"José, is it?"

"Yes, madame."

"Don't 'madame' me. My name is Gwendolyn. There's a guest bedroom below the stairs to the attic, where I sleep. Be sure to make the bed in the morning so that no one will notice you've slept there. You can go up now, or you can share some port with me while we admire my latest work. We can talk about art if you like. Giles tells me you're a specialist in Paula Rego's artwork. I'd be very interested in hearing your take on her. I promise I'll keep my opinions to myself, which is the best thing to do when conversing with an expert on any subject."

They discussed Paula Rego and Botticelli's two versions of the Birth of Venus. His brief presentation on Rego's art was so encompassing and insightful that she begrudgingly admitted there was more to her art than caught her eye.

She noticed José worked out lifting weights and was in excellent shape. She marveled at the idea that an artist would work out. No wonder Giles snapped him up. He behaved as a perfect gentleman, not once flirting or even looking meaningfully into her eyes. He certainly cut a fine figure, so unusual in the artist world. But not now. She would have time to play on some remote beach resort soon enough.

As for her, she was simply exhausted and relieved to finally accomplish what she set out to do. It was several months of low-boil stress. Without George and his goons, it would have been as comfortable as her childhood summers at her grandparents' house on the New Jersey shore. That, plus the two of them finishing the remaining half bottle of Rui's port, started her yawning.

"Hey, José. Let's call it a night. We can get up early, have a simple breakfast, and be out of here by 0900."

Gwendolyn showed him his room and continued up the stairs to her own. José chose to lie on the bedspread with his clothes on, to avoid messing up the bed. She locked the door and took one last look at the garden in the moonlight. Quickly undressing, she fell into bed. She was asleep as soon as her head hit the pillow.

CHAPTER FOURTEEN

A black van quietly parked in front of Rui's house. A lone lamp emitted a dim light from the living room. A voice seething with hatred hissed, "There! There she is! I've found you, my little one. You're mine now." It was George.

A sycophantic voice came from the back seat. "Wow, boss! You're a genius. How did you know?"

"I'm not a genius. I'm simply smarter than all of you combined. It's simple. My dear friend, Rui, told me. We had a falling out at our Venus ritual when we had it at his home last. Ironically, our argument was about the red demon who is in that house at this very minute. But a few weeks later, I called him to make amends. We did and during that call, he told me his plans to go upcountry to visit his cork tree harvest. It was then I ended your bumbling attempts at trying to catch her. And that, my followers, brings us to the present moment."

"He told you she was here?"

"No! He didn't tell me she was here. I knew that already from seeing her at our ritual. But what I wasn't expecting was how easily an amateur artist girl could outsmart and lose my best, most talented grown men. I can only assume that you fools are even more amateurs than she is.

"But I'm willing to overlook all of that now. As I can see that Rui's Land Rover is not here, that means neither Luisa nor he is here, either. So, then, who could that be in his house with the lights on? Any guesses? No, don't guess. I think I know who. We will wait a bit after the lights go out and we shall claim our prize. In the meantime, make sure the syringes are ready."

"Boss, how're we going to break into the house without waking her?"

"My dear trusting friend, Rui, gave me the keys years ago and forgot to ask for them back. Leave the details to me. Doc, you double checked that the Versed, Ativan, and Valium proportions are correct? We need to have her unconscious inside two minutes."

"Yes, Sir George. They are exactly correct and ready, just as you commanded. Make sure to inject her where there is little fat, like her wrist or forearm. You know I won't help you. I'm only an advisor, remember?"

"Of course, I remember. OK, here's the plan. Team A will come with me to the back where she might slide down the drainpipe as she did the last time I was here. Team B will silently go in the house, climb the stairs to the attic, and try to enter her room. Remember, do not break the door down. If it's locked, pick the lock. Make some noise. I expect that would compel her to flee out the back window, where we'll be waiting for her.

"Whoever encounters her first, remember how the good doctor showed us how to administer it, in the wrist or forearm, as he said. First you need to immobilize her. You won't be able to inject it accurately if she's able to move her arms. There's four of you in each team. I certainly hope you can overpower her. Any questions?"

"Boss, why would you not let us do a drive-by shooting weeks ago and be done with it?"

"A what? A drive-by shooting? Are you crazy? This isn't Los Angeles. We're civilized here in Europe. Besides, I need her for a special ritual, a special celebration to our Mother Goddess, which requires many steps, including a full moon, which luckily, we'll have in three nights. And all of you are invited to attend. It will be spectacular, I promise.

"Oh, look! She turned out the light. Now, she's going up the stairs. There! She switched on the attic light. OK, it's out, too. We'll give her fifteen minutes to fall asleep and in we go. When I say the word, we'll open the gate to the driveway and back in the van as silently as this electric motor will allow. We must not leave any sign that we've been here. Nothing damaged. No marks. Nothing. Got it?"

Eight voices spoke in unison as schoolboys would, "Yes, boss."

Fifteen minutes slowly crept by. George looked up from his watch. "OK, show   time, folks!"

George unlocked the large gate. Two others slowly pushed it open, stopping after the first rusted squeak.

"Hey, you. Oil those hinges!" George whispered.

After they followed that order, they continued opening the gate without it complaining. The van backed in so that its front was just outside, hiding it from casual eyesight. George opened the front door with his keys and showed Team B the stairs for them to ascend. He led the others to the back, where he was confident that they would finally capture her. There they hid in the shadows of the bushes. Everything was prepared. George's heart pumped with excitement. He lived for moments like this.

Team B quietly climbed the stairs with a small penlight to guide the way. Suddenly, a step creaked. They all froze. They heard nothing in response, so they continued. But the creaks of the gate and the footsteps had not gone unnoticed.

The creaking gate woke both José and Gwendolyn. She dismissed it and went back to sleep. José thought it strange and lay awake staring at the darkness of the ceiling above him. But the creak of the stairs had him on his feet, alert to the intruders. He hid in the corner by the door.

They opened every bedroom door to make sure no one could surprise them from behind. Their unsuccessful attempts to remain silent would only succeed with someone sleeping, not with someone wide awake, who could hear each doorknob turned and each footstep made. Finally, his door opened and an arm with a penlight extended into the darkness.

José grabbed it and pulled the intruder off balance and into the room. He fell on the floor, dropping his penlight. José was on top, beating him. They rolled around on the floor in the darkness, scrambling for an advantage. The three others of Team B at last could hold José still, and one of them stuck his wrist with the syringe. He yelled to Gwendolyn that she was in danger, to run and escape. As the drug took effect, José fell limp and unconscious, sprawled across the carpet.

Despite that surprise, Team B had accomplished their mission. Gwendolyn suddenly sat bolt upright when she heard José yelling. She quickly dressed, opened the window to the terrace, and stepped out. Clouds obscured the moon, but she did not need light to know where the drainpipe was.

She slid down the pipe and was immediately grabbed by George's team. She could not budge from their grip. A hand tightly covered her mouth. Then she saw George leering in her face.

"I caught you, my little rabbit. You fell right into my trap. The big bad wolf has caught his prey, fair and square. Now go to sleep. We'll talk in the morning. Sleep tight." Then, from the light of a penlight, he found her vein on her wrist held tightly immobile and injected the syringe. She struggled, then went limp in under two minutes, as planned.

"OK, we have what we came for. Steven, climb up and make sure her room appears as if she simply packed and left on a whim. Close the window and unlock her door. I can hear those fools trying to pick the lock all the way down here. Tell them to meet us at the van."

Steven climbed up the drainpipe and entered through the open window. He unlocked the door and closed the window. Not one to make his own bed, he certainly would not make hers. He grabbed her knapsack and followed Team B to the van with their unconscious José.

Both teams met at the van and put their two unconscious captives in the rear. George confirmed the front door and gate were properly locked. The van left as silently as it had arrived, all within five minutes.

George, sitting beside the driver, leaned back, and sighed with satisfaction. He had her. Finally, he had the means to make the spirit of his Mother Goddess smile on him. In only a few short days, the world will have one less red-haired demon.

"Hey, boss. Brilliant plan! We did it. But what should we do with this other one we caught?"

George was startled out of his reverie. "Who the hell is he, anyway? Does anyone have any idea?"

No one had a clue. This wrinkle to his plan perplexed him for a moment. Was he a lover? No, they would have been in the same bed. That would have been a major complication. A guest of Rui? But Rui told him on the phone he had no guests staying there. Was Gwendolyn not a guest? Never mind, he would take that up with Rui later.

After a few moments, George decided what to do with the stranger. "Doc, prepare a deadly cocktail and send him to the great Beyond. You two will bury him in the old graveyard when we return. But be careful with the girl. I have plans for her, grand plans."

They drove on the highway for about forty-five minutes and then took an exit to increasingly narrow country roads, barely lit by the pale moonlight. Fenced in fields stretched over the rolling hills on both sides of the decrepit farm lanes. Finally, they arrived, first passing what was once the tall main entrance that was now blocked by an ancient, rusted gate lost to the world of functionality. They continued around to the other side of the compound that required scrambling down a bumpy dirt trail with brambles and prickly vines scraping the sides of the van.

The van stopped in front of a metal gate locked by a chain and a heavy padlock. One of them jumped out and opened it. The van entered and parked next to the relatively undamaged barn. Everyone climbed out. The clouds had temporarily opened, and the moonlight shone through, revealing the collapsed farmhouse about fifty steps from the barn.

The old decrepit farmhouse was long ripe for demolition. The roof had caved in. The windows lost their wooden shutters years ago. Rubble and fallen, decayed wooden beams filled most of the interior of the two-story farmhouse. The dwelling was once the home of a family of eight, with six bedrooms and spacious living quarters on the ground floor. But no one had stepped into the house for over fifty years. It was surrounded by twenty-six hectares of farmland overgrown with waist-high weeds.

The two, whom George instructed earlier to dispose of unlucky José, retrieved shovels from the barn. Doc opened the rear of the van and gave the syringe to one of George's lackeys to administer the deadly injection. After five minutes, Doc confirmed he was ready for burial. The two with shovels handed them to a third, who followed as they slowly carried him across the back field to a collection of old crumbling family tombstones under an old oak tree on the opposite side to the gate. They found a level patch of ground somewhat out from under the tree, allowing the moon to illuminate the burial.

Hidden from the outside view and down age-worn stone steps was a thick wooden door dug into the ground that gave access to a basement. It was here where George made his Portuguese temple to his Mother Goddess, Venus. He had other temples in various other countries spread around the world, but this was the main one, the one to whom all the others owed allegiance.

They carried the unconscious Gwendolyn, who had the dubious luck of not being snuffed out at once, down into the dark dank temple of horrors to a cell in the far back corner. George instructed several of his followers to undress her and put a white robe on her. While the others held her up, Steven undressed her, pausing to admire her beauty in all its glory. He could not help holding her breasts in his coarse hands, gently squeezing them.

George smacked him hard on the back of his head. "What do you think you're doing? Would you like to join the stranger under the oak? This is not a woman. This is a sacrificial lamb being prepared for slaughter. Do you understand?"

Rubbing his head, Steven nodded, though his blood still rushed with desire for the sweet unblemished lamb. They dropped the white robe over and placed her on the stone slab covered in a thin layer of straw sewn into a makeshift blanket that was her bed. After covering her with another similar old straw blanket, they filed out, and locked the cell door.

A guard was posted outside the door. They left the sole ceiling light on so they could check on her through the small iron-barred window of the cell door to make sure she would not try to hang herself. They had already removed anything that could serve as a noose, but yet... One could never be too sure about the creativity of the condemned in their attempts at self-destruction.

The horrors of Gwendolyn's nightmare had begun.

CHAPTER FIFTEEN

From the small iron-barred window high in the cell wall, the late morning sun shone on Gwendolyn's face. Many families of birds had made their nests in the ruined farmhouse above the cellar. Their chirping gradually intruded into her slumbering consciousness.

Still half asleep she wondered how she had wound up on the hard bedroom floor. The previous night's nightmare was just too terrible to ponder. Finally, she opened her eyes to a ceiling full of dusty cobwebs, supported by large, rough-hewn wood beams. She sat up with a shriek. But immediately fell back in a swoon.

The guard called for his boss, who wanted to be present when she awoke. George hurried over with several others. He swung the cell door open and stepped closer to his prisoner. Many of his henchmen filled the doorway, hoping to witness how their first interaction would go.

"Easy, my pet. Take it easy. You'll be better in a few hours. Would you prefer I return later?"

Turning to her side, Gwendolyn saw the person addressing her. She immediately covered her face and screamed.

"Fine, then. I'll see you later. If you need water or something to eat, just tell the guard."

They left, slamming the heavy door shut. She eventually stopped screaming a few minutes later. She had a pounding headache, her mind filled with blind panic. Her nightmares finally caught up with her. For a moment, she believed she had died and was in Hell. George the Devil was there to meet her. Had she lived such a terrible life to deserve this? True, she was an art forger and a party to stealing expensive art. But surely that was not so bad as to deserve the endless torments of the Inferno?

Slowly, her headache subsided, and the chirping of the birds became more noticeable. Reality reasserted itself as she realized she had neither died nor was in Hell. She struggled to sit up and assess her predicament. They had locked her in a square cell twelve paces from stone wall to stone wall. The floor was stone as well. The window, located just below the ceiling, was too high for her to look through.

A stone basin sat below a rusted spigot against the far wall that only produced smelly brown water. Beside it was a wooden bucket to serve as a toilet. They had dressed her in a roughly woven linen robe that hung below her knees. Trapped as a prisoner, she had nowhere to go.

George had won. He had her in his clutches. She could not appeal to his sense of mercy. He clearly had none. Certainly, he was criminally insane. He told her he would return later. She had to figure out the best approach to escape her plight. What that would be, she had no idea.

*****

George returned to his private rooms. He sat at his desk to review the year-to-date reports of the cult's worldwide progress in ridding the world of the redheaded representatives of the Great Satan on earth. His temples were in thirty-seven countries around the world, on every continent. So far that year they had made twenty-three sacrifices. The Florence chapter had been most active.

Then there was the report on the near misses. These always made him angry. How could they be so stupid to let any of them escape? With just a little planning and thoughtful action, it should be a simple thing. He personally never let any get away. After rereading the report from the Peru chapter, he just shook his head. How could they let one escape by jumping off a cliff into the river below?

*****

Two hours later, the cell door opened and in stepped George.

"Ah, so good to see you're up and at 'em. I trust you slept well. So sorry about the accommodation. This is the only available guest room we have at the moment. Over the years, I've built quite an impressive temple. Come, let me show you. I must admit, I'm more than a little proud of my creation. You two, Bring her with me."

Two men grabbed her under her arms and lifted her off her feet. They followed George with her feet dangling in the air.

"Now, little lamb, take a look all around you. Isn't this one of the most impressive houses of worship you have ever seen?"

The first thing she noticed was a tall statue of a woman at the far right end of the room. Slightly above her head perched a halo of dancing flames. She had a flowing white robe reaching to her feet. Her arms held a baby boy. She resembled a Renaissance Madonna with Child, except for a single horrible fact. Rather than a serene face, she had a demonic one like Kali, the Indian Goddess of Death. Her mouth was wide open in an insane grimace, revealing a crimson tongue and fangs. Another attribute added to the dread: she had long red hair.

In front of the grim idol stood a roughly hewn stone altar with a smooth top surface coated in dried blood. Blood stained the floor surrounding the altar. A butcher's table in an abattoir would have been less bloody. Rows of loose wooden benches extended to her left, almost reaching the door to the outside. Along the walls and surrounding the bloody Madonna were tall, thick crimson candles on wrought iron stands. The scent of the candles could not mask another smell. It had a strange metallic coppery tinge. Gwendolyn remembered from her past reading of horror novels that it was the smell of human blood.

If it were not for the men holding her, she might have fainted when she saw what hung in large   mesh sacks above the altar. The two sacks were full of heads, shrunken heads. The eyes and mouth of each were crudely stitched shut with thick black thread. She groaned when she noticed what they all had in common. Their red hair was completely entwined together, drooping down like Spanish moss from the old trees of the Florida swamps.

After giving her the time to take in the horrors, George broke the silence. "Oh, I see you appreciate my handiwork. I carefully, nay, lovingly prepared each of those beautiful heads. I learned that from a few followers I have in Peru. You can't imagine how much work it takes.

"First, I must sever the head. After boiling it for an afternoon, I must then remove everything that's inside, including the skull. I have to cut it into smaller, manageable pieces, and remove them with forceps. Only the skin on the head remains. At this point, it looks kind of like an excellent quality Halloween mask. Then I sew shut the eyes and mouth. Next, I place hot stones inside the head. That's what does the shrinking. Finally, after I take out the stones, I sew up the neck after it has taken its final diminutive size.

"It requires real skill. I had to practice on pig heads until I got it right. Unfortunately, I'll not be able to give you a live demonstration as it will be your head I'll be working on next.

"There, you see? Those were all your sisters. I correct myself. They are still your sisters, and they are waiting for you to join them. And you will! You'll join them and your new mistress, the great Mother, where you and your sisters will share the duties of serving and pleasing her for all eternity. And soon, so very soon! We are merely waiting for the Moon Goddess to reach her perfect size and shape in two nights. Luckily for you, you only need to wait mere hours. A few of your sisters had to wait for weeks until our goddess was ready to accept their sacrifice. I am so looking forward to this!"

Despite the apparent utter hopelessness and horror of her situation, the absurd caricature of evil insanity that George presented made her laugh. It was not a jolly laugh, but rather one full of disdain and ridicule. She had inadvertently discovered how she should react to her tormentor. She would taunt him into seeing how ridiculous he was. The chink in his armor was his complicated relationship with Rui.

Her laughter was so contrary to what he was trying to accomplish, George speechless as he tried to process her strange reaction. Laughing at him in front of his followers? This he could not tolerate. He reacted in precisely the worst way. He lost control and slapped her right before them. "Put her back in her cell, damn her! We'll soon see just how funny this will be for her."

The men holding her returned her to the cell and roughly dropped her on the cold floor. The door clanged shut behind them as they left her to her misery. She rubbed her still-stinging face. The early morning sun crept across the floor. Time was slipping by.

Gwendolyn sat on the stone ledge that served as her bed and only seat. She took stock of her situation. She was solidly locked away at an unknown location. With less than two days remaining, she had to figure out how to escape. The only things she had were her white robe and her wits. It was not much, but it was all she had.

The only thing that seemed important to George was Rui. But how could she connect these two dots? She pondered this for about fifteen minutes when he suddenly reappeared at the cell door window. He had regained control of himself and came back to turn the tables and taunt her.

"After more time for contemplation, you likely grasp the revered and serious nature of the honor I have bestowed upon you. The very thought should fill your heart with joy. Don't you agree?"

"Agree? You're a pathetic excuse for a man. You're no man at all, but a stereotypical woman-hating fairy. A real man would respect a woman and not create ridiculous amusement park horror houses to torture her. You should go back to your merry old England where you upper class degenerates can play at whatever fantasies you have in the safety of your isolated mansions."

"How do you know anything about me?"

"How do you think? Rui told me all about you."

"Rui told you? Why would he do that?"

"I don't know. Why don't you ask him? While you're at it, ask him what he thinks about you kidnapping and threatening his special friend?"

George went silent at that, his face a shade paler. In a flash, Gwendolyn found the connection between the dots. It was her. She would use Rui as a lever to pry open the crack that was slowly expanding in George's head.

"This is not about Rui. It's about the majestic Mother Goddess. It's far greater than him. Besides, he joins me in our worship of her. He welcomes us into his home to express our respect and reverence for the great Venus."

"The Mother Goddess? What a joke! He thinks it's just a silly farce. He and all of your other fellow Venus lovers understand her for what she really is: a lustful goddess of physical pleasure between a man and a woman."

"You lie!"

"Where do you see a mother in all of this? Venus is clearly not a 'Mother Goddess'. That's just plain crazy. She is the Goddess of Physical Love, not an object of maternal religious devotion, but of physical beauty and, yes, sex. Is this how you remember your own mother? Was she a hateful, murderous monster like your ridiculous statue? She had red hair, too.

"Why do you hate us redheads? What would she think of your obscene behavior? She was angry at how your father treated her. Like her, you, too, should focus your anger at your father, a dishonorable, abusive man, not innocent young redheaded women. Well? Explain yourself!"

George screamed, shaking the metal bars of the window. "You know nothing! You're making up lies. They will not save you!"

"Lies? Lies? It's the truth and you know it! Rui told me. He wouldn't lie about something so serious. It is you who is lying. Lying to yourself."

"Your master, the Devil, he's taunting me! No! I will not listen. We'll meet tomorrow night and then we'll see how you feel as you stare at the abyss." He turned to walk away. Gwendolyn panicked that she may have lost her chance.

"Rui doesn't care about you anymore. He hasn't cared about you for decades. It's me he wants. It's me he desires. Me! Do you hear me? It's me!"

George returned to the cell door window and laughed. "You? Why would he want you, an ugly redhead? You're lying to me again." He shook his head and started to walk away again.

"Really? Me, an ugly redhead? Well, how about I prove it to you? I can prove not only that he desires me, but also how he really feels about this sacred Venus of yours."

That completely caught George's attention. He pressed his face between the bars. "You can prove it? How so? This better be good."

"Oh, it's better than good. Since you have the keys to his house, you can easily prove it to yourself. You know his artist studio in the garden. Go there and you'll find his own version of Venus, which he is still painting. But you'll see enough to get the idea. Oh, there is nothing maternal about it.

"How do I know? Because he's painting me as his Venus rising from the sea. Her face and nude body are my own. I was the model for it. He specifically asked me to look at him with the same desire and lust as the Venus above his fireplace looks at him every night as he drinks his port. Any normal man can notice that, except for you. The photo he took of me posing nude for him is taped to the wall next to the painting. Go there and you'll discover the truth. The likeness is unmistakable."

George's pale face turned purple in rage. He shook the bars. He banged his head against the door. "You liar! Yes, I'll go and see for myself. But if you're lying, I shall personally torture you all the way to tomorrow at midnight, when you will beg for death. Yearning for it."

"And what if I'm right? What then? Will you release me?"

"Release you? No, but I'll make your death quick and painless. How about that?"

"You'll see! He looks at me with lust in his heart. He desires me, not you. You're nothing more than a court jester to a king. He ridicules you. Deep down, he despises you!"

George screamed again, then abruptly turned and left. She smiled. She got to him.

Gwendolyn leaned back against the stone wall and stared at the cobwebs in the corners of the rafters. Gradually, her smile disappeared. How could enraging her tormentor help her situation? She considered the alternative: playing the innocent lamb preparing to be slaughtered.

That is exactly how he considered her, calling her 'lamb' every chance he got. The other victims must have meekly gone to their executions sobbing all the way. She simply could not do that. If it was her time, she would go kicking and fighting. If she could shake the confidence of the evil little prick along the way, all the better.

CHAPTER SIXTEEN

Rui kept his Piper PA-28-180, a four-seat single-engine plane, at the local Cascais airport at Tires, a short fifteen-minute drive away. He parked by the hangar and loaded the dogs in the back seats with the luggage in the storage space below. Luisa sat beside him as he carefully maneuvered his plane to the runway. After a brief wait, while he checked all his controls, the control tower cleared him for takeoff.

Gathering speed down the runway and ascending into the sky was one of his favorite things to do. Passing over Lisboa below, he followed the Tejo River northeast. As he approached the historic city of Santarém, he turned due east toward the Spanish border. He landed on his own private airfield.

One of the cork harvesters met them at the small hangar with an all-terrain vehicle. Rui loaded the luggage and Luisa into the vehicle. He preferred to walk with the dogs the ten minutes to his spacious wooden lodge. With no need for leashes there, he let them run loose. From door to door, the entire trip took a little over an hour.

After helping unload the few items of luggage, he and the worker left to see how the cork harvesting was coming along. Luisa stayed behind to open up the lodge and unpack. The dogs galloped behind the vehicle as it slowly made its way deeper into the cork groves. A few hours later, both Rui and Luisa joined the workers for a communal lunch at the barracks near where the cork bark was semi-processed into usable long wide strips for the wine bottle cork stopper business.

In the afternoon, Rui continued his inspection in a different direction for the rest of the day. As the sun set, he returned with the exhausted dogs to wash up and prepare for a wonderful dinner with his mate on the wide veranda overlooking the western valley. He greatly relished Luisa's cooking on these trips. Her rustic Alentejo roots would shine as she prepared the hearty cuisine of her grandparents.

Candles flickered between them as the last rays of the sunset shone before them. Rui made sure his lodge was always well-stocked with the local Alentejo wine. Luisa did her best to create a truly romantic moment. Normally quite jovial at these jaunts away from home, Rui was quiet, almost morose.

She pulled him into conversation by asking how the harvest was coming and what the quality of the cork would be for that year. Rui appreciated everything she did for him. He did his best to be his typical, cheerful self. She just figured he was tired, not being as young as he used to be. She said as much, and he agreed. His years were working on him. Because of this, they went to sleep early.

But all night, Rui tossed and turned. He rose and roamed the moonlit house. He went back to bed again. But he could only get snatches of sleep. He was so restless that Luisa gave up and went to sleep in one of the guest rooms. The early dawn found Rui staring at the ceiling, clearly disturbed by something. He got up and headed outside to chop firewood. Even that could not calm him. Luisa heard him and rose, too. She busied herself preparing breakfast.

They had breakfast in a small sunroom on the east side of the house. The cork trees blocked the sunrise, but an occasional sunray peeked through. Rui did not look well.

"Rui! What is the matter with you? You hardly slept at all last night."

"Yes, my dearest, I just couldn't sleep. Something gripped my heart and gave me a strong feeling of dread, of some kind of foreboding. I simply can't shake it. I'm afraid I'll be quite useless on this trip."

"Ah, Rui, for heaven's sake, what's bothering you?"

"I had no idea until I started chopping the firewood. Then it occurred to me. It's Gwendolyn."

"Gwendolyn? Why on earth would she bother you so?"

"I'm afraid, Luisa. I'm very afraid that something terrible will happen to her while we're gone. It's driving me crazy."

"What could possibly give you that idea?"

Rui was silent, staring at his now cold eggs.

"It's George, isn't it?"

Rui closed his eyes and cringed.

"You didn't tell George about our trip, did you?"

Rui remained silent.

"Rui! No! You didn't tell him!"

"Unfortunately, I did, Luisa. Now I regret it. Even so, I can't believe he would do anything to her. What could he do, anyway? She seems to be someone who can take care of herself. Defend herself against George if it ever came to that."

"Oh, Rui, when will you grow up and leave that pile of damaged goods behind you?"

"You're right, Luisa. Of course, you're right. But we go back a long way, he and I."

"Not again! How many times have I heard you say that? And now you're ruining our holiday together because of an unspecified anxiety you're having about him. So, what now?"

"I'm so sorry, Luisa. I simply cannot concentrate on anything else. I'll be useless to my workers and worse, useless to you as your loving mate. I need to return, just to put my aching mind to rest. You can stay here if you want. Almost certainly there's nothing to it. If so, I'll be back here in time for lunch with you."

"Alright, Rui, fine. I'll go back with you. Round up the dogs and I'll pack up."

Twenty-five minutes later, they were airborne. Rui flew in silence, becoming more anxious the closer the plane came to arriving at the airport. He had to remind himself to occasionally check his flight instruments to make sure the tachometer's RPM needle stayed out of the red zone.

Finally, they arrived. Luisa told Rui that she was driving. He was simply too nervous to drive a car. Rui constantly urged her to drive faster. At one point, annoyed, she stopped the car. He understood her point and controlled himself enough for her to continue home.

As soon as she parked the car, Rui jumped out. The front gate stood open. He rushed in and then froze. George sat on the grass with legs spread, leaning against the studio wall. His eyes were squeezed shut. His face distorted in a grimace. His hands gripped his head. A low moaning was barely audible from where Rui was standing. Luisa followed Rui in with the dogs on their leashes and saw the same.

Rui instantly became clear-minded. He whispered to her to take the dogs inside and check if Gwendolyn was there. If not, go to her room and see what she could find there. Yell down from the window what she discovered. George had not noticed their arrival. Rui waited the few minutes for Luisa to go through the house.

She opened the window of Gwendolyn's room, causing Rui to peer up at her with a quizzical look. Her face was heavy with worry. She shook her head. "She's not in her room. But she must be around here somewhere. She never leaves without making her bed and it's not made. Where else could she be?"

"Or she was suddenly taken against her will." Rui approached George seething, fearing the worst. George did not notice Rui standing over him until Rui hit him hard on the side of his head, knocking him over onto his side in the grass.

"Hey you! What the hell are you doing in my house? How did you even get in?"

George whimpered, more emotionally hurt than physically. He slowly rose from lying on the grass and returned to supporting himself against the studio's wooden wall.

"Answer me! I'll tell Luisa to call the police, as you are nothing but a common criminal, a common burglar trespassing."

George abruptly stopped his pathetic moaning and whimpering. He looked up, his face suddenly went dark. His anger overcame his mental confusion. Gwendolyn told him the truth about everything, including the polaroid of her pinned to the wall, posing nude with an expression full of desire and lust.

"You! You betrayed me! I was right. She was here during our ritual, spying through the window. How could you let such a lecherous fiend stay with you? How could you allow her into your house, even for a moment?

"Betrayed you? How? I never promised I would have nothing to do with a woman. I never promised you anything! She was a guest at my home. What did you do with her? Where is she!?"

"You know how I feel about them, those redheaded monsters. And in your studio, what is that? You're defiling our goddess with your lewd and blasphemous painting! I am so disgusted with you." George unexpectedly sprang up to attack Rui. Rui threw him hard against the studio wall. He collapsed back onto the grass.

"Look, you damn bastard, I'm the one asking the questions. You attack me once more and I'll break you in half. You're such a seriously crazy idiot, living in your own strange world. All of us can see that my Venus is not the pure, demure virgin as the one in the Uffizi.

"Mine is exactly the same as I paint her, a lascivious, lustful woman full of desire, just like in the painting above my fireplace. Our rituals, as you call them, are nothing more than off-beat parties for middle-aged men with imaginations fueled by booze and wild sex. You're the only one who thinks it's a religious experience of a non-existent cult. Back on topic. How did you get in here and where is she?"

"You gave me the keys once a few years ago and never asked them back. I was supposed to take care of your dogs while you went on a trip to Morocco."

"Give them to me now!" George dug into his pocket and reluctantly handed over the keys.

"Where is she? George, what did you do with her? I swear if you have done any harm to her, I will personally tear you apart, limb from limb. Answer me!"

"Why do you think I have anything to do with her being gone? Maybe she tired of you and left, like I did?"

"You left me? You left me? What the hell are you talking about? I left you! You sobbed and begged on your knees for me to stay. You cried like a baby as you clung to my shins. I should have cut off all connections with you, instead of agreeing to your pitiable plea to remain friends. I don't care about any of that. Gwendolyn! Where is she? She would not have left without saying something to me. You must have her somewhere."

"Me? What makes you think I have her? What would I do with her, besides what she deserves?"

"You have her! Everything points to you!"

"You can't prove a thing. Your accusations are baseless nonsense."

"George! For the last time! Where is she?"

George remained silent as he seethed in anger. Suddenly, Rui grabbed him by the throat and squeezed. George struggled against the much stronger and bigger Rui, but to no avail. Rui started banging him against the studio wall, while George desperately tried to pry Rui's hands from his throat.

Luisa ran down the stairs to grab Rui and pull him away. "Rui! What are you doing to the worm? Throw it out and never let it back in. He's not worth spending the rest of your life pacing the walls of a prison cell."

Rui slowly loosened his grip as he realized the wisdom of Luisa's words. He suddenly swung around behind George and put him in a choke hold. "OK, Luisa. Fine. Open the gate so I can throw this pile of trash out into the gutter where it deserves to be."

Hardly able to hide her joy, Luisa did so. Rui manhandled the loathsome deviant out onto the street. He threw George hard face first into the side of his black van, leaving a dent in the door. He rolled on the pavement, holding his forehead. His right eye was already swelling, forcing it half shut.

"I don't want to ever see you again! Luisa was right. I should have thrown you out of my life forty years ago. There, now I've thrown you out. You're out, do you hear me? You're out of my life forever!" Rui was nearly shouting.

Luisa muffled his mouth with her hand. George struggled to his feet and entered the car. He drove away, shocked and dismayed at how things so quickly spiraled out of control.

He had driven like a cheetah to Rui's house, nearly causing several accidents along the way. Now he crept back to his horrid lair. Again, he almost caused accidents, but this time by driving below the minimum speed limit. His mind was sunk in a black fog. He did not notice the many cars honking their horns at him as they passed.

Two hours later, he parked in front of the barn. He was surprised to see a team of his men with scythes cutting down the tall brown grass and weeds behind his ruined farmhouse. He stopped and asked the one acting as the foreman what they were doing.

"Why, boss, don't you remember? You told us you want to plant grape vines here. Only yesterday you told us to cut the weeds to do this. Are you alright? What happened to your face?"

George ignored him. He had to put some ice on his eye and lie down. He turned and entered his hidden temple. Several others inside noticed the state he was in and rushed to his side. "Boss! What happened to you?" they yelled with genuine concern.

This made Gwendolyn curious. She looked at the sorry sight through the cell door window. She laughed. "Hey you, little man! Everything I told you is true, isn't it?"

George had to admit she was. "Yes, dear lamb, you were right. According to our bargain, I promise you won't feel much of anything for very long. I really wish you were wrong. Oh, how I wish you were wrong, but a deal is a deal."

"This story isn't over yet. Ooh, you look bad. What happened to you? Did you run into Rui? Looks like you ran into something. Rui must have returned home concerned about me, and he found you there. Obviously, it didn't end well for you. I suppose you aren't friends anymore. Rui will find me. He'll save me, you'll see!"

George raised his eyes to the ceiling and screamed, "Why? Why are the demons tormenting me?" He hurried to his room and slammed the door shut. Quickly grabbing a bottle of pills, he poured a few into his hand, and swallowed them. He filled the bucket with ice water and placed it by his bed. After soaking a washcloth in it, he placed the ice-cold compress on his swollen eye. Confusion, anger, regret, frustration, even fear raced through his mind.

He was completely unable to understand what just happened with Rui, the gentle easy-going, always kind-hearted friend he had for most of his adult life. Sure, they had misunderstandings, even spats at times, but he could always make Rui relent in the end. Rui was his friend, probably the only one he had.

Yet, how could Rui make a pact with the Devil's representative on earth? Rui lied to him about the redhead staying in his home. That was bad enough, but what possessed Rui to create such a blasphemous caricature of the great goddess? Clearly, the redhead called a demon to possess Rui and pollute his mind. Could it be that easy? Could she do the same to him?

Why were things not going as smoothly as they invariably had in the past? Certainly, the goddess made things easy for him, each time opening a trouble-free path to her sacrifices. It was as it should be. After all, everything he did was for her. Why is she not looking out for him as she always had before? Maybe she wanted to tell him something. Perhaps it was Rui who had fallen out of favor with her, and this was her way of communicating that to him? George could not believe she would be so cruel as to take his only friend from him. This recentered his anxiety back on himself.

He broke into a cold sweat as he considered that he might be losing her favor. How could that be? He was her steward on earth. He sent her a long line of servants to keep her comfortable and happy. Serving her was the only thing that gave his life meaning. Finally, worked up to a frenzy, he screamed: "Mother! Do not forsake your only son!"

He fell unconscious back onto the pillow. The pills took their effect.

CHAPTER SEVENTEEN

Giles paced back and forth in his hotel room. He looked at his watch for the twelfth time in five minutes. It was 1020 and there was no sign of Gwendolyn. She was rarely ever late, usually early for their appointments. If something came up, she always called. He had already called her five minutes ago, but no answer. He called her again. Still nothing. He called José. No answer either.

What could have happened to her, to them? Did she find José appealing after all? Did they fall madly in love with each other and run off to the Riviera together? Giles refused to believe that. Gwendolyn was the most solid, clear-headed person he had ever met. She was way too responsible to miss an appointment. She would have called at least. Had her phone died? How could José's phone have the same problem, too?

He considered taking a taxi to Rui's house to see what happened. But then, they might cross paths on the way. If she had fallen down the stairs or otherwise, José would have called. None of it made any sense. By 1030, Giles was anxious, calling once every two minutes.

Still no answer. Could she be ignoring his calls? He could not believe that. Suddenly, his eyes fell on her bags occupying a chair by the window. Maybe something in her luggage could help. He did not want to go through her things, but he was already desperate.

He opened her top smaller bag. He felt around for a card or note paper. What was that? His fingers touched a card. He pulled it out and indeed it was a calling card. It was Rui's. It had his name, address, and phone number. Giles decided to try one more time calling Gwendolyn before contacting Rui.

*****

The pills calmed the screeching voices in George's head, and he slowly regained consciousness. They could not help his pounding headache and swollen face. The ice pack helped, but it was not enough. He had been trying to stay off the painkillers because they made his mother's whispers more sinister than they usually were. He closed his eyes and hoped for sleep.

Suddenly, a cellphone's piercing ring broke the silence. Five minutes later, it rang again. Then it rang every minute or so. Enraged, George slammed open his door and yelled for someone to bring him that offending cellphone.

"Please boss, it's not ours. It belongs to the redhead bitch. It's ringing from her clothes."

"Bring it to me!"

They dutifully brought her phone and clothes to him.

He grabbed the offending phone and threw the clothes back. "Burn the clothes!"

George sat down at his antique baroque wooden desk and stared at the phone, knowing it would ring soon. It did.

He answered it and yelled, "Stop calling! She can't come to the phone now. Not now, not ever!" He suddenly burst into laughter, the laughter of the mad. He picked up a heavy wooden mallet and smashed the phone repeatedly to pieces.

Gwendolyn had heard her phone ring from the first. *So, it must be after 1000, maybe 1030 by now. Giles is trying to call me. He'll find me. Either he or Rui, or both of them will come to my rescue. They must!*

*****

Upon hearing the hysterical upper class English accented voice answer, Giles screamed into the phone, "Who are you? Where is she? What have you done with her?"

But the phone was already dead after the first smashing sound. Reaching for the nearest chair at hand, he collapsed into it. He was so shocked by the devilish voice and laughter; it took him several minutes to recover his senses. He broke out into a cold, panicked sweat.

That accent! That upper class English accent of natural superiority, Giles heard it every day at his boarding school from all his teachers and classmates. It could only be one person. It was George! He had her. What could Giles do? Finding Rui was his only option. He dialed the number on the calling card. Giles' heart raced as it rang. Rui answered.

"Hello?"

"Is this Rui?"

"Yes. Who's calling?"

"My name is Robert. I'm a close friend of Gwendolyn. We were supposed to meet for brunch an hour ago. But she never showed up. I'm seriously concerned about her."

"Gwendolyn, did you say? How do you know her, and how did you find me?"

"I'm her ah… uncle. She gave me your phone number, in case anything happened to her. I'm extremely worried that she is being held captive by a friend of yours: an Englishman named George. She told me about him. I've been calling her with no answer, maybe fifteen times.

"Finally, a crazy sinister man answered with an English accent. He told me that she could not come to the phone and never would. Then he smashed it. What do you think he meant by that? Has he killed her? We need to find her and him, too! Rui! We must do something!"

"Yes, yes, it is George. Where are you now?"

"I'm staying at a hotel in Lisboa. I can take a taxi and be at your place in about half an hour. Do you know where he is and where he may be keeping her? What does he want to do with her and why? Is she even still alive?" Giles' voice was becoming frantic.

"Look, calm down. Unfortunately, I know George. He has very strange, sick really, ideas about redheads. He is seriously insane. I caught him in my garden just now, acting extremely suspicious. He thinks he's the leader of a secret cult that worships a painting of Venus I have hanging in my living room. Never mind that. What matters is that he never does anything important unless there's a full moon. The next one is tomorrow night. So, I believe she's still alive.

"I don't know where George is exactly, but I have an idea of the area he may be in. He mentioned to me a few years ago that he bought a farm about an hour north of Lisboa. If he has her, that's where they both are. I have a small plane. We can try to spot the farm from the air. Get over here as soon as you can, and we'll look for her."

Giles rushed out of the hotel and jumped in the first taxi in line. He seriously doubted they could find her from the air. The alternative was to search every farmhouse in the area, which was clearly impossible. It was his only hope, and he was surprised to find himself praying for the first time since he was a child.

*****

Rui considered what to do while he waited for Gwendolyn's rather odd uncle to arrive in about a half an hour. Luisa made sandwiches to get them through until dusk. She asked him why not call the police to see if they might help. He laughed sardonically at the idea. But then decided it could not hurt. He dialed the emergency number for the police.

"Good day. Your name, address, and the nature of your emergency, please."

Rui gave her his information and then paused about the nature of the emergency. "The nature of my emergency is a missing woman, probably kidnapped."

"Describe the woman in question."

"Well, she's in her late twenties, an American artist from the US. She's tall, slim, with red hair."

"What is your relationship with this missing... artist?"

"My relationship? We're friends."

"Friends?"

"Yes, just friends."

"Dear sir, from the sound of your voice, I'd say you're well past seventy. Am I right?"

"Y-y-es. And so what?"

"Has it occurred to you that this 'just friend' might have grown tired of you and left for greener pastures?"

"Greener pastures? What are you talking about? Your job is to take down the information and report to the police to find her!" Rui was losing control of his anger.

"Sir, don't tell me what my job is! If you continue being rude, I'll have to hang up. Or if you prefer, I can charge you with breaking Decreto-Lei Number 62/1978, which states: it is a crime to be rude or disrespectful to a public servant which may lead to six months in jail and, or a 10,000 Euro fine. Now, which would you prefer?"

"Look, you... OK, OK, fine. Let me talk to your superior."

"He's very busy. You can talk to me. Let's start over. What's the nature of your emergency?"

"Look, she is a US citizen. If something happens to her, the US Embassy will not be happy about it, especially when I tell them I contacted the police, and they wouldn't help her."

"Now, now, sir, no need to get testy about it. I'll see if he's available."

While Rui waited, he noticed he was pacing up and down his back garden, extremely agitated. A few minutes later, a man's voice spoke.

"Commissioner (police lieutenant) Antonio Carvalho speaking. You mentioned that maybe a US citizen is in trouble. How can I help you?"

"Yes, Commissioner Carvalho, I had a guest in my home, staying here while she searched for a place of her own to live. She disappeared. I think she was kidnapped. I'm afraid something terrible happened or will soon happen to her."

"OK. Let's start with what do you know? What makes you think she was kidnapped and not gone of her own volition?"

"It's completely not like her to leave without saying anything."

"How long have you known her?"

"About three or four months."

"Hm, that's not so long. OK, for the sake of argument, do you have any idea who might have absconded with her?"

"Yes, yes, I do! It's George!"

"George? OK, who is he and how do you know him?"

"Let's just say he's an old acquaintance from the UK."

"So, how can you be certain that he took her?"

"Because her uncle called the young woman's cellphone, and George answered it."

"Her uncle? How does he know George?"

"He doesn't."

"So, why does he think it was George? Did he introduce himself when he answered? Why would he do that, unless he and the girl are very close for one to answer the other's cellphone? Senhor, you're not helping me."

"I know it was George. Who else could it have been?"

"Let's just assume for the moment that he did take her against her will. Where could they be now? Do you know?"

"No, but I have an idea that they are at a farm not too far north of Lisboa."

"At a farm somewhere north of Lisboa? Is that the best you can do? Even if we could, do you expect us to search every farm? My dear senhor, I'm afraid you have not given me anything to work with and I'll have to agree with Senhora Leitão's assessment. US citizen or not, I really have more pressing things to deal with."

Hit by a flash of inspiration, Rui interrupted him. "Senhor Commissioner, have you heard about the murderer of redheaded women in Italy that was recently in the news?"

"Yes, senhor. What's your point?"

"My point, Senhor Commissioner, is that I think George is exactly this same serial killer. My young friend is a redhead."

"A redhead, you say?"

"Yes, sir. Imagine if George is indeed the very same and you bring him to justice. Why, you would be world famous! Journalists will beg for interviews. Your chief would have no other choice but to give you that generous promotion, one which I'm sure you've been waiting for a very long time. Everyone will want to be your friend, sports and movie stars, everyone. You'll appear in magazines and on TV. They'll name streets after you. Your wife would be so proud of you. Your children..."

"OK, OK, I get it. Fine, I'll help you. But you need to help me help you. So far, you have given me nothing that is actionable. What do you want me to do?"

"OK, great. I promise you won't regret this. This George, who I know has a pathologic hatred of redhead women, told me he bought an old farm a few years ago about an hour or less north of Lisboa. Obviously, I agree we can't search every farmhouse. So, my plan is this. Her uncle will arrive here any minute. I have a small plane at Cascais airport. We'll fly over this area and search for anything suspicious. If we find anything, I'd like the police to be available to immediately search it."

"Strange, but now that you mention it, there have been several unsolved cases of young foreign women disappearing. We found no sign of them and just assumed, to close the cases, that they simply returned home. I seem to remember that some were redheads, too. Hm, most of them were, come to think of it.

"OK, senhor, you have my attention. If you find anything suspicious, I mean truly suspicious, call this number that I'm about to give you. It's my direct line. I'll contact the local police station for that area, and we'll investigate. What might you find that would fit that description?"

"Not sure about that. However, I do know that he drives a large black van, something that no farmer would have. That would be worth investigating."

"Yes, that would. Alright, senhor, I'll wait for your news. Don't forget what you promised me. If you do forget, I can make life very difficult for you."

"Oh, no sir. That's the furthest from my mind. Ah, here comes her uncle now. I have to go. We need to start searching right away."

"OK. Good day and good luck!"

CHAPTER EIGHTEEN

While Rui was still talking to the police commissioner, Giles arrived and rang the gate bell. Luisa led him into the house. Giles could not help glancing at Gwendolyn's wonderful rendition hanging above the fireplace as he passed the living room. This only increased his anxiety even more.

Rui finished his call and hastened to greet Giles. "I just got off the phone with the police. They will help us only if we can identify the correct farmhouse. Luisa prepared a bag of lunch and bottles of water for us. So, let's get going. Do you need to use the restroom or anything before we go? Once we're in the air, we can't make any rest stop."

"I'm good to go now."

During their short drive to the airfield, Rui could not contain his curiosity and asked, "Robert, right? Where are you from? You sound very English."

Giles replied, "Yes, that's correct. I'm from England."

"I must say you speak English with the same accent as George does: upper class boarding school English. I detected none of that with Gwendolyn."

"Yes, well, clearly, I'm from the English branch of the great oak that is our family tree. Sorry if I sound like him. There's many of us who speak this way. It's considered quite the asset from where we come from. Jobs are offered or declined based on one's accent alone."

"Well, never mind. I learned my English in similar circumstances, rising up through the English public boarding school system, though I started the good breeding process only after I was thirteen. I suppose some would consider us members of the upper class of Portugal. We only have ex-nobility here, or worse, nobility wannabes. Most Portuguese would laugh if I told them about my family background. Most, but not everyone. Those who would not mind are the ones who only offer one cheek when they meet, as opposed to both cheeks, like everyone else does here."

"Now don't get me wrong, Rui. I'm in no way a member of the upper class. My father served in the RAF and was based around the world when Britain was still great. He compensated for his not being available to his son by putting me in the English boarding school system from year one. So, my proper Queen's English was his greatest gift to me. My parents spoke English as it's spoken in working class Newcastle."

"Fine. We all have to be born somewhere from someone. After all, we can't choose our parents. Here's the airfield now."

They parked near the hangar. While Rui was refueling the plane, Giles did his best to empty himself in the restroom. When everything was ready, Rui opened the small door to the back seat. "You sit back here. That way you can search from both sides. Here are the binoculars. Put this headset on. Once we're airborne, it'll be too noisy to talk without them."

Rui taxied to the runway. As he waited for permission to take off, he continued. "Remember, we have only one chance to get this right. If we find a place that looks suspicious and we're wrong, the police won't give us a second chance. We must be as certain as possible. Can you shed any more light on this terrible thing?"

"Not much. She had told me that for a few weeks a month or more ago, various men were trailing her during the day. So, I guess he has many others involved in this."

"So, maybe if you see a farmhouse with many cars parked nearby. I also know that he drives a large black electric van big enough to carry ten or more. That's something a farmer wouldn't have either. That would be a definite sign, too. Besides that, simply search for anything else suspicious.

"I'll fly at around 500 meters (about 1600 feet) of altitude in a zigzag pattern on the western side of the highway that runs north from Lisboa, bisecting the area where I think George is. The western part is almost half the size of the eastern half. So, we should be able to cover it in an afternoon. If we find nothing today, we'll have all day tomorrow to cover the other side."

"And if we find nothing tomorrow, either? What then?"

Rui remained silent, as he had no answer. "OK, we have permission to take off. I'll tell you when to start looking. Let's go find this young artist in distress!"

About ten minutes later, Rui's voice came crackling through Giles' headset. "OK, start looking now. For the most part, because I'm flying in a zigzag, you can just look out the right-side window. If you notice something, let me know and I'll fly back over it to give you a closer look."

Giles pressed the binoculars tight to his face and peered down to the rolling hills spreading before him. He eagerly hoped to discover something suspicious at the first farm they flew over. But no such luck. After an hour, the only thing different between them was what they were growing in their fields. Some were vineyards, others were orchards, some were even growing vegetables, but most were wheat fields.

The farmhouses with their barns were all nearly identical. The houses all had red-tiled roofs and pictures with religious or historic scenes painted in blue on white ceramic tiles built into the walls. Small gardens separated the main house from the fields. The barns were like barns anywhere, large nondescript utilitarian buildings where they stored the tractors and other farm equipment. Near the barns were piles of old junk such as tires, broken toilets, stacks of wooden boards, various plastic things, etc. that could be used for an unknown purpose at an unknown future time. After all, one never knows when one might need a broken wheelless wheelbarrow.

Once Giles sat up with excitement when he saw a farmhouse with four cars parked haphazardly near the barn. He told Rui, who then dipped lower over the area of interest. His excitement turned to dismay when he noticed that one of the cars was sitting on cinder blocks without wheels. The other three looked as if they were nearing the same fate as their forlorn, ignored wheelless brother.

Rui confirmed through the headset. "No, those are typical farmers' vehicles. George wouldn't let his followers drive cars like that. The shame of it! Keep looking."

After another hour, he told Giles that it was time for lunch. He would fly in a circle so Giles could enjoy his lunch without his binoculars being attached to his face. Besides, he needed to rest his eyes, anyway. After eating the delicious sandwiches Luisa prepared, he leaned back in the cramped uncomfortable seat, trying to stretch his legs the best he could. He closed his tired eyes. Ordinarily, he would have nodded off to recharge his mental batteries, but his anxiety about Gwendolyn would not allow it.

Rui reached back and nudged Giles, who immediately sat bolt upright. "What? What! Have we found her?"

He handed Giles a plastic bottle with a funnel in the neck. "No such luck during our quick lunch break. Here. I almost forgot. If you need to urinate, use this. I can't help you with the other end. Are you OK with that?"

"Ah, thanks. I didn't have any breakfast, so I think I'll be fine with that end. I've finished those excellent sandwiches; so, I'm ready to continue searching."

Rui resumed flying north on his zigzag pattern. Giles continued peering below, desperate for any sign that could be interpreted as a lair of Gwendolyn's enemies. It was late afternoon, and the sun was casting longer shadows. His eyes strained to see clearly in the advancing dusk.

Rui's words broke through the increasing gloom of Giles' mind. "We've run out of possibilities for today, Robert (Giles). Over those hills are bedroom communities for Lisboa sprawling further to the north. No farmhouses there. It's getting dark. We'll have to return. It would be better if you spend the night at my place, so we can start again tomorrow as soon after daybreak as possible. What do you think?"

He sighed OK. Rui continued, "I'll fly back right through the center. You can take another look while we return to the airfield."

Giles did so, but there was nothing different below. Tears filled his eyes as he thought, "Oh, my dearest, Gwendolyn! What have I got you into this time?"

Rui landed and taxied to the hangar in silence with his heart filled with dread. They exited the plane. He noticed that Giles' eyes were red and wet from tears.

Rui grabbed him by the shoulders. "Look, this is no time to despair. George told me that his farm was an hour's drive from my house north of Lisboa. There is only one area where that could be. We covered about a third of it. Tomorrow we'll cover the rest. We are certain to find her."

"Yes, but what if I don't notice anything and we fly right over her?"

"Oh, I doubt that. George would not be content to leave things as he found them. He'd make some obvious change to give himself away. I'm sure of it."

"Like what? I need to know what I should look for."

"I really couldn't say. He simply isn't one to leave things well enough alone. He needs to put his mark on everything, kind of like a male dog in that way. All I can tell you is you'll know it when you see it."

"If you say so." Giles could not hide the doubt in his voice.

Back home, Rui showed Giles the bedroom he would sleep in. Dinner was a silent affair. Sitting before the fireplace sipping after-dinner port wine was a friendly gesture, but the more he looked at Gwendolyn's painting hanging so beautifully in front of them, the more he had to fight the sadness welling up inside his heart. It was better to remove himself from it and go to sleep early.

Rui agreed, as he was in no mood for conversation, either. His feelings swung from fear for the safety of his newest friend, whom he took into his home but could not protect her, to shame that his erstwhile friend was the cause of their turmoil. The whole thing exhausted him.

Giles took a shower. Not bringing anything in his rush to meet Rui that morning, he washed his socks and underwear, draping them up to dry above the bathtub. The bedspread was dusty, but the sheets were crisp and clean. He threw the bedspread off and went to bed. As much as he tried, sleep was impossible, as terrifying thoughts raced through his mind.

After an hour, he gave up and got out of bed. He wrapped a towel around him and decided to search for any telltale sign, any hint of José and Gwendolyn. Rui and Luisa were already asleep, judging from the noises coming through their respective bedroom doors. Giles tried the door of the vacant room across from his. It opened.

With his cellphone to light the way, he noticed the carpet was in a mess from people rolling on it. All the furniture was knocked out of position. He surmised that José, surprising them, must have tried to protect her. The bedspread was still wrinkled from him lying there. Giles smoothed the carpet and bedspread. He put the furniture back into their proper places to hide any sign that someone had been there recently.

Next, he ascended the stairs to Gwendolyn's room. Her bed was disheveled, too. But at least that made sense. She was always meticulous with everything she did or was involved in. If she had the time, she would have carefully made her bed while her captors waited. Unfortunately, they clearly did not have the patience to wait.

Giles searched throughout the bedroom and bathroom. He even turned the lights on to see better. He could discover no sign or clue to help them find her. As he spun around to return to his room, he spotted the painting of the yacht by the sea hanging on the corner wall. Its style was without a doubt hers. That must have been what caught the attention of Rui that fateful day when this all started. Tears rolled down his face as he returned to his room.

"Oh, Gwendolyn! Where are you, my friend?"

CHAPTER NINETEEN

Gwendolyn nervously paced between the walls of her cell. It was some time after her satisfying interaction with her captor. She had slipped back into despair. She tried to piece together what had happened. Most likely Rui was worried and returned home to check on her. As luck would have it, he discovered George there. Their meeting apparently did not go well for the murderous maniac.

What could she conclude from this? Rui found his long-time friend trespassing in his house, but that in itself would not have turned violent. It could only mean he must have suspected George had something to do with her disappearance. What would he do about it? What could he do? He had to find a small, ruined farm among a hundred before midnight of the next day. Even if he did, he was only one frail old man against dozens of thugs.

She sat down, depressed at the utter hopelessness of her situation. Even worse, she had neither eaten nor drunk anything since the night before. She hesitantly walked over to the worn mossy stone sink and turned on the rusty spigot. Smelly murky water trickled out. Not daring to drink from it, she returned to her stone bunk.

Gwendolyn was condemned to die at midnight the next day. Why would she fear getting worms or whatever other diseases might exist in the putrid water? She considered the logic of the choices. She thought of the condemned Burmese prisoner, avoiding a rain puddle while being led to the gallows in George Orwell's story, Burmese Days. Like Orwell's prisoner maintaining his human dignity to the end, she decided she would rather die of thirst but with her dignity intact than be debased retching in her diarrhea.

What did she have to lose? She spoke through the cell window to the guard on the other side. She asked for water and something to eat. He sneered at her, asking why would an already fatted lamb need to eat more before its sacrifice? Gwendolyn could only think to reply that the goddess would prefer an even fatter lamb to a thinner one.

He returned about five minutes later. He thrust a plastic cup of water through the door window, followed by a toothpick. "Fine. Here's a cup of rainwater and a toothpick. You know, just in case."

"What am I supposed to do with a toothpick?"

"If you don't need it, then eat it." He laughed as he stepped away.

Gwendolyn gulped down the water, then threw the cup against the cell door, accompanied by a long list of expletives. What could she do with the toothpick? She could not really use it to stab herself in the wrist. It would simply not work. Besides, would she do that, anyway? She realized she could not and laid down on her straw mat. Her mind was racing in despair, with nowhere to go.

Later, she turned to her side and watched the sunlight creep across the floor. Her mind went blank by the time the dusk's gloomy remnant of light shrouded everything in a somber hue. There had been several changes of her guard. One of them switched on the cell light. As weak as it was, it dazzled her eyes. She sat up. Night had fallen. Still no Rui or Giles smashing through the doors.

She rose and looked out at the night sky. Judging by the position of the moon peeking out from the clouds, she guessed it was somewhere around 23   00. She heard two guards talking outside. One was relieving the other. There was silence for another twenty minutes. Then a leering face filled the cell door window.

"Hey, you, little lamb. You must be starving. Come over here closer. I'll give you a half a loaf of bread if you lift up your robe and show me everything."

Gwendolyn reacted with disgust. She looked away, not concealing her disdain for his offer.

"Hey, look. I have it right here." He showed her a fairly large half loaf of bread.

While she turned and glared at him, she considered what this unexpected turn of events may mean. It was a desperate chance. But she had to take it. Her snarl slowly turned to a smile. She sauntered over to him, swaying her hips under the robe.

"You clearly appreciated a fine, womanly body. You must be the only man among these crazies. Would you like to touch my warm softness?"

"Oh, yes I would!" He panted as his groping hands reached towards her through the cell door window.

"Well, then, you'll just have to sweeten the deal."

"Yes, yes, OK. What would do it for you?"

"Let me out of here and you can come with me. We can spend some good times together on a lonely, romantic beach. Would you like that? Can you imagine my nude body next to yours, snuggling against you?"

He went quiet as he considered that wonderful offer. Finally, he whispered, "As much as I would love to do that, I can't. George and his flunkeys would hunt me down like hounds on a doe. Besides, there are two armed guards at the only exit to this place, one inside and the other outside. How could I smuggle you out without the whole place coming alive with crazies? It'll have to be something else, something I can realistically do for you."

"What else can you do for me?"

"Hm, well, you know you only have until tomorrow night. Wouldn't you like to experience some physical pleasure one last time? You know, enjoy the sensation of my manly strength inside you bringing you to your final climax?"

"If that's the best you can come up with, then you can shove your manly strength up your ass."

"OK, OK, look, I'll tell you what. How about I give you a decent meal? I can give you what we had for dinner. I mean, clearly, I can't order a pizza to be delivered, but we had grilled salmon. I could heat that up for you, plus everything else we had. How does that sound?"

It was Gwendolyn's turn to be silent. After thinking for a moment, she answered. "Oh, why not? Throw in a few bottles of cold beer to wash it down with and you have a deal."

His face changed into delight. He could not believe his luck. She agreed! He disappeared. Gwendolyn noticed outside the door the lights were out. Only the many candles along the walls flickered dim light into the dark center. Faint snores were coming from the other side of the horrid room. Collecting her thoughts, she prepared for his return. She had no idea what she would do, but she was confident that something would occur to her when the time came.

He came back around ten minutes later with three beer bottles tinkling against themselves as he hurried back with a full plate. He was at least clear-headed enough to only bring a harmless spoon for her to use. Unlocking the door, he entered, closing it behind him. The fragrance of the hot salmon and fried potatoes filled the cell, masking the otherwise usual dank stench.

"Give me the food and stand over there while I eat it." Gwendolyn motioned to the far side of the cell. He obediently handed the still warm plate to her and set the opened beer bottles next to her. He removed himself to the indicated place and watched her with a face full of lustful desire. His eyes greedily followed her every movement and curve of her body as they teased him from under the loose robe. Memories of her nude body were already arousing him. She would be his soon.

She wolfed down the food. It was not a lot but was enough to satisfy her hunger. She sat back and sipped a beer, all the time considering her next move. Making him wait, even for another minute, would make him rash with impatience, as the blood of his one head flowed to the other.

"OK, big guy. I'm ready for you. Come here, come onto me. We can finish the other two beers afterwards."

As he quickly approached her, he unzipped his pants. She pulled her robe up, exposing her maidenly beauty to him. He stood between her open legs and dropped his trousers to his ankles. He placed one hand on her breast and prepared his member with the other. As he leaned over her, she suddenly grabbed him by the collar of his shirt and slammed his head hard against the stone wall above her.

He recoiled back from her, stunned, nearly unconscious. His pants around his ankles made him fall backwards. When the back of his head hit the stone floor full on, he went silent. His glassy eyes stared unseeing at the ceiling. He was dead.

Gwendolyn stopped to listen for any sound coming from outside of the cell. There was none. She quietly opened the door and peered out at the exit at the end of the large open hall. What was the guard doing? He was not there! Maybe he went to the toilet. She crouched low and quickly approached the great heavy wooden door that opened to freedom.

She noticed that her little knapsack was in the corner by the door. She detoured there and slipped it on. Her running shoes were beside it, the ones she wore when she slid down Rui's drainpipe. She quickly put them on, as she could not run far in her bare feet.

After slowly opening the door, the cool night air hit her face. The outside guard was smoking a cigarette, staring at the cloudy night sky. His rifle was leaning against the wall. He did not see her when she grabbed his rifle and hit him squarely against the side of his head. He groaned as he fell to the ground. At that moment, the inside guard, returning to his post, saw what had just happened. He yelled to alert everyone that the prisoner was escaping.

Gwendolyn did not wait another second. Glancing at the locked gate near the barn, she dropped the rifle and ran towards the sprawling tree over the ancient cemetery on the opposite side to the gate. Its wide branches hung over the high wall topped with barbed wire. Her fluttering white robe made her look like a shimmering ghost as she clambered on top of an old tombstone to reach one of the lower tree branches.

A guard picked up his collapsed comrade's rifle and aimed to shoot her down like a squirrel from a tree branch. One of his mates grabbed it and pointed it to the ground. "Are you crazy? We need to catch her unharmed! The boss will flay us alive if we don't bring her back safe and sound!"

They ran to the gate and fumbled at the lock before they could open it. A more responsible one split them into two teams. He ordered one team to go around the farm to the right and the other to the left. They would use their cellphones to communicate. One called the other, and the other answered. Without hanging up, they could inform each other of their progress tracking her.

The two teams ran in their appointed directions. Between clambering over walls and stumbling through neighboring fields, the going was slow for them. Gwendolyn only had a few minutes head start, but unlike them, she ran with the speed and grace of a gazelle.

CHAPTER TWENTY

Gwendolyn did not wait for them to sort themselves out. She dropped down from the cemetery tree branch into the cornfield on the other side, disappearing from their view. By observing the sun during the day, she knew which way south was. Being unconscious during her abduction, she had no idea where she was.

If she was north of Lisboa and the River Tejo, heading south would get her there. If she was south of Lisboa and the river, well, at least any direction away was better than staying put. She just needed a goal to run to, anywhere far from the temple of terror.

She ran across the two hectares of the field and leapt over the low stone wall that marked the beginning of the neighboring farm. Panting heavily, she slid down against the cold stones of the wall. Knowing her cellphone was in George's sick hands, she opened her knapsack anyway, where she found her special knife that she normally wore strapped under her right forearm. She carefully secured it to its proper place under the sleeve of her robe. Being spring-loaded, the blade was normally hidden safely in its sheath until Gwendolyn released it turning her right hand into a deadly weapon.

It had saved her life many times in the past. After releasing it once by mistake while she was sleeping, almost killing herself, she always took it off before she went to sleep ever since. Perhaps if she had been wearing it when George had paid her his unwelcome visit, she would not be in her current predicament.

Suddenly, she heard the shouts of the men searching for her. She leapt to her feet and began running again, this time through a wheatfield. Unlike a cornfield where she could run in any path between the rows of corn, a wheatfield would reveal exactly in what direction she ran as the crushed wheat stalks formed a trail behind her. She had no choice but to continue.

The night was dark until the moon shone its silver light between the gray moving clouds. She passed through a few more fields of various types of agriculture. She did not hear voices anymore. So, she decided to try her luck with one of the gloomy farmhouses. She banged on the back door until a lamp came on within. She shouted for them to open the door and let her in.

A man's frightened face appeared in a window. He disappeared and opened the front door, releasing his barking dogs into the front yard. As they ran around the house to the back where Gwendolyn was, she sprinted to the dividing stone wall of the neighboring field, leaping over it just before the dogs caught her.

Panting on the other side of the baying hounds, she wondered why he did not help her. As she regained her breath, she realized from his point of view that a white wraith-looking she-devil banging on his door in the middle of the night shouting a strange demonic language might have given him a heart attack.

The crazed dogs desperately trying to jump over the wall could indicate her location to her pursuers with their frenzied barking. She continued running this time through rows of grape vines attached to their trellises, leaving no trail behind her.

After alternating between sprinting and resting, she finally came across a narrow country road. She picked a direction and continued her escape. At last, she found a crossroads where a café bar was still open with the lights on inside. She could not believe her luck. She stopped before the door, took a deep breath, and entered.

The lights were dim. Old European football club pennants and posters of past players covered the bare walls. Beer bottles and mugs with various smaller shot-sized glasses for aguardiente crowded the simple white plastic tables. The Super Bock beer supplied these and the matching plastic chairs in exchange for a monopoly on the beer on tap in the dingy café. It was a café because of the large espresso machine that dominated the space behind the bar.

There were about twenty men scattered at the tables watching a Brazilian soccer/European football game. Judging by how they were dressed, they were local farmhands. As soon as Gwendolyn closed the door behind her, they all turned to stare at her. Gawked might be a better word. First, she was a woman who would never be in a bar by herself at that hour. Second, she was still wearing her white robe.

Ignoring them, she strode to the bar and asked the bartender to use the phone. He did not understand her English. She spoke the word 'telephone' slowly and loudly. He simply shrugged his shoulders and shook his head. The café did not have one. She turned to the shocked men and asked loudly over the TV noise if anyone spoke English.

Only gaping mouths with blank expressions answered her. In the corner, one ruffian suddenly elbowed his friend and whispered in his ear. He answered her, "Excuse me, Miss. We speak English. What do you need?"

Gwendolyn rushed over. "I need to use a phone. May I use yours?"

"My phone? I suppose so. But the signal is terrible in here. We'll have to go outside. Come, follow us."

The other one threw a few Euro notes on the table as they rose and led her to the door. Outside, the one with the phone was staring at it. "Still no signal. Over here, it seems to be stronger." He led her to the side wall of the café away from the street. "Who do you want to call, anyway? Is it outside Portugal?"

She was impatient to call the police. "No, no, just the police."

"The police? Why? What's the matter?"

"I've been kidnapped. I escaped and now they're chasing me."

"Kidnapped? Really? Who would do that way out here in this farmland?"

"How would I know? Just give me the phone! They could be here any minute."

"Fine. Here." He nodded and the one standing behind her suddenly pinned her arms and held her tight against his chest. He quickly replaced his cellphone with a pistol. He placed the muzzle squarely against her temple.

"Well, it's your lucky day. We are the police around here. You could say we work for a private security company. The office is very close to here. We can go there now to file your complaint."

The other one finally spoke up. "Hey, Rob. Why don't we do her right here before we take her back?"

"Nah. Too risky. We'll have our chance tomorrow night after the ritual."

He noticed Gwendolyn's shocked bewilderment and explained in more detail. "Oh, I doubt you know about our local traditions here. You see, after the Boss cuts out your heart, he allows us to have our way with the sacrificed lamb's still warm body. In ancient days, they used to eat the flesh of the sacrificed animals. But we're not so barbaric as they were. The Boss will be so pleased with us for retrieving his lost lamb that he'll surely give us first dibs. You probably wouldn't know this, but if you're the fifteenth man in line, things can get pretty nasty down there."

Gwendolyn gasped in terror. She had managed to find two of George's madmen, even after her successful escape. She was so close, so damn close! This new bit of horror flashed in her mind. She considered for a second that she could open her knife into the heart of the one behind her, only to be shot in the head by the one in front. Which would be the better way to go? She still had hope that Giles or Rui would save her. So, she wavered.

The one holding her pushed and otherwise manhandled her to a nearby parked car. He threw her roughly into the back seat. The one with the pistol got in beside her, pressing it against her ribs. The other drove the short distance to the horrid, ruined farmhouse. They were greeted as heroes by the cheering team of fellow followers, who were frightened out of their wits by George's reaction if he discovered his lamb had fled her cage. They acted like the condemned on the scaffold who were unexpectedly pardoned by the king.

Their joyous cries brought George out of his fitful slumber. He was beside himself when he saw Gwendolyn standing in a circle of his cheering minions. The two who recaptured her told him their story.

"Good work, gentlemen. You will be properly rewarded when the time comes. Come, put her back in her cell. Let's find out what happened. Who was on guard when she escaped?"

The one who passed as a foreman hesitantly replied, "Ah, I think it was Steven, sir."

"Steven! Where is he?" The answer became obvious when they entered the cell. "Well, well, well, Steven. Why are you laying on your back staring at the ceiling with your pants around your ankles and your willy on display? What do you have to say for yourself? Well, answer me! Explain yourself! ... Oh, nothing to say, huh? We'll see about that."

Everyone else standing behind him gave each other furtive glances. No one dared to tell their all-knowing leader that the fool was dead.

George continued. "Still nothing to say? OK, fine. Hey, you guys. Take him outside, strip him, and tie him to the pillory. We'll see if he persists in being unable to explain himself then."

They dropped Gwendolyn on her stone bed. George looked at her with embarrassment. "I'm so sorry, little lamb. Really, I am. You must feel simply horrified by your ordeal. No matter. You are safely back where you belong. I'll double the guard, so nothing like this happens again. They'll keep each other in line. You must be famished. I'll make sure you get more bread and water."

George instructed them to clean the cell up and feed her a half a loaf of bread and more rainwater. Several of them lifted Steven's body, revealing a small puddle of blood under his head. They carried him outside to the stone pillory George had specially built only a few paces from the door. They normally are found in medieval town squares in front of the church where those deemed mildly criminal were tied, beaten, and left for days.

He followed them out. After they securely tied Steven's body to the stone pillar, George asked for one of the long, sharp butcher's knives from the kitchen. After it was dutifully proffered, he stood facing silent Steven.

"Well, how about now? Anything to say in your defense? ...Of course, you have nothing to say. There is nothing you can say. You're a disgrace to me, to your brother believers, and most of all, to your goddess. Let's see how you'll react to this."

George sliced off his so-called 'willy'. "First, we must remove the cause of your sin against your goddess. See? Now, you'll never sin again, at least with this. You must be relieved already. No reaction? Not even a cry? That's alright. We shall continue."

He continued by slicing off his ears, then his nose, and proceeded after an hour to flay the dead body completely. He imagined himself as the imperial executioner of the Celestial Empire, administrating the death by a thousand cuts. A copy of an old photo stuck on the wall by his desk showed a condemned Chinese man tied to a public pillar where a pair of imperial executioners with knives in hand were already well into the process.

The idea was to cut off just enough flesh each time so that the condemned could live until a thousand cuts could be made. It was a typical traditional Chinese hyperbole. They rarely survived past a hundred. The poor victim in the old photo, held up by Imperial guards on each side, was clearly alive, still standing, though his eyes were staring blissfully from a heavy dose of opium. Part of his arm was already gone. George had a fertile imagination.

Exactly as in George's photo, the crowd surrounding the spectacle were both shocked and fascinated by the horror they were witnessing, as was normal with all public executions from the dawn of organized society. As for Steven, after George was through with him, there was nothing left but a pile of bloody flesh around his bony feet.

CHAPTER TWENTY-ONE

Giles had finally fallen asleep from exhaustion. Six hours later, he dreamed that he was banging on a heavy wooden door. He could hear Gwendolyn singing on the other side, but she was not opening the door. Was she not able or not willing? He pounded and shouted at her, becoming ever more anxious.

Then he heard Rui answer from the other side, but it was him pounding on the door and not Giles. For over a minute, Rui had been banging on Giles' bedroom door, yelling for him to wake up. Giles finally awoke and answered.

"OK, OK, I'm awake now."

"Fine. It's already 0700. Time to get ready. I want to be in the air before 0900. Breakfast is on the table. I'll meet you down there."

Giles pulled himself together. He dressed himself in his still-damp clothes and headed downstairs. He was groggy with only about five hours of sleep, but it was nothing several espressos could not manage. Fortunately, they had an espresso machine. His grogginess turned to anxiety when he realized that, according to Rui, this was the last day to find their young friend. He was fully awake when that realization sunk in.

Giles forced himself to eat the generous breakfast Luisa prepared. Rui ate very little. He rose suddenly and told Giles it was time to go. He needed no reminding. Luisa handed them a paper bag with their lunch and bottles of water on their way out.

In the car, Giles broke the heavy silence, "Say, Rui, what will we do if we find them?"

"I'll call my contact with the police and return to the airfield. We can't land on these uneven fields or narrow country roads. We'll meet them there and go rescue her."

"…And what if we don't?"

"If we don't? I don't have any idea what else we can do. I really don't…" Rui's voice trailed off.

They arrived shortly at the airfield. While Rui was preparing the plane, he told Giles, "Better use the restroom here. We could be in the air for thirty minutes or nine hours. You know we only have empty bottles."

"Fine. I'll be right back."

When he returned, Rui already had the plane prepared to enter the runway. Giles climbed in the back and put on the headset. He grabbed the binoculars and braced for takeoff. Soon they were in the air on their way north. Rui flew over the north-south highway that divided the two search areas. The day before, the west side produced no results. Their only hope was in the larger eastern section.

Rui's voice came through Giles' headphones, "OK, we have arrived at the southern end of where we'll search today. Like yesterday, I'll fly in an east to west zigzag pattern. Let me know if you see anything. I'll fly lower to take a closer look. Let's find this girl!"

The first thirty minutes turned into an hour, then into hours. There simply was nothing suspicious below. Each farm looked like the last one; each more mundane than the one before. As much as Giles wanted to tell Rui to fly lower around a particular farmhouse, there was truly nothing unusual about any of them.

The sun was starting its descent when Rui told Giles that they would eat lunch while he flew in a narrow loop. Though he was not hungry in the slightest, Giles' eyes really needed a rest. He ate little of the sandwiches Luisa had prepared and rested his eyes for a quarter of an hour. During the whole time, he could only see Gwendolyn in his mind's eye. It was simply too much.

His eyes snapped open. "OK, Rui, I'm ready to continue."

More hours passed. Giles still could find nothing that was close to being suspicious. He noticed the shadows were becoming longer. He glanced at his cellphone. It was already 1500. He asked Rui how much time they still had. Rui answered that they only had around two hours of fuel left. They needed about half an hour to reach the airfield. That meant about ninety minutes at most. Giles' heart was pounding. He whispered to himself, *Come on, Gwendolyn! Come on! Where are you? Please show me something, anything!*

Half an hour later, he was beside himself. Sweat trickled down his cheeks. His heart thumped. Time was running out. Then it appeared, a farm very different from all the others.

Though they had flown over dozens of empty, ruined farmhouses, even with collapsed roofs, this one was different. For one thing, there was a line of men with scythes were cutting the weeds behind the house. Why would anyone do that on an abandoned field? And scythes? Who uses those anymore?

There were outlines in the earth under their feet of two by one meter/yard ovals, spaced apart at regular intervals in neat rows of five by four. The oval closest to the ruins was an empty hole with a mound of dark earth beside it. The old family cemetery spreading below the oak tree a short distance away had a freshly dug and recently filled hole. As they passed over the barn, Giles saw the large black van.

"Rui! I think I found it! Fly lower over that farm again! Those look like graves down there, maybe twenty of them."

"Yes, there's his black van! Here's my cellphone. Take photos as I fly over them. I'll go as slow and low as I can, but I don't want them to get suspicions."

Giles took the cellphone and took a dozen photos with maximum zoom. The men in the field looked up as he photographed them. Their surprised expressions meant that was all the time Rui could take.

He turned the plane south to return to the airfield. He took his cellphone back and called Commissioner Carvalho. The commissioner answered after two rings.

"Commissioner Carvalho speaking."

"Good day, Commissioner Carvalho. This is Rui Silveira. I called you yesterday about a missing redhead woman. Well, I think we found her! We flew over a ruined farmhouse with what appears to be many graves in a field behind it. There are a dozen or more men cutting down the weeds above this grave site with scythes. There is the same black van as George's parked beside the barn. I'm telling you, Senhor Commissioner Carvalho, she must be down there!"

"Calm down, Senhor Silveira. What are the coordinates?"

Rui read off the coordinates from the plane's GPS system. "As soon as we hang up, I'll send you the photos that we just took. The evidence is clear that something very suspicious is happening down there. I mean for one thing, there are nearly two dozen graves arranged in neatly spaced rows."

"Graves? Really? Better investigate it. Let's see. That's in the jurisdiction of Salvaterra de Magos. So, here's the plan. We'll pick you up at Cascais airport and drive over there to meet the Salvaterra police. We'll go rescue this girl together."

"Yes, Senhor Commissioner Carvalho. We'll be there in about half an hour."

"Fine. Stand outside the entrance to the terminal. We'll pick you up from there."

Twenty-seven minutes later, Rui landed and parked the plane in the hanger. Giles hopped out of the back seat even before it stopped completely. His legs were unsteady from sitting in a cramped space most of the day. Once Giles could walk steadily, Rui signaled for him to follow.

It was a five-minute walk to the small, sleepy terminal. With only ten flights a day, little activity occurred. They stepped outside the airport entrance across from a sparsely filled parking lot. Within five minutes, a police car approached them and stopped. It was Commissioner Carvalho.

"Ah, you must be Senhor Rui Silveira. It's a pleasure. And you? You must be the uncle. A pleasure, too." Carvalho greeted Rui and Giles, shaking their hands in turn. Giles did not understand his Portuguese, but nodded, anyway.

Carvalho was a mid-level police officer in his early forties. His career was anything but meteoric. It was more of a plod. Being polite and following procedure would normally bring one to a desk job sooner or later. What Rui offered was the most exciting thing in his whole twenty-two years on the force, or in his whole life, in fact.

A younger policeman stood next to Commissioner Carvalho. "Oh, this is Principal Agent (police corporal) Oliveira. He's our driver today."

Oliveira shook their hands and spoke to Giles in quite good English, "How do you do, sir? Pleased to meet you." Giles replied in kind.

Carvalho ignored him and continued, "Senhor Silveira, I looked at those photos you sent me. They certainly are suspicious. We'll go meet our PSP (public security police) colleagues just off the highway exit closest to those coordinates you sent me. Until we know for sure what we're dealing with, we'll keep the GNR (national republican guard) out of this. Come get in. We can talk on the way." He opened the back door for them.

Immediately after the doors were shut, Oliveira hit the accelerator hard, turned on the siren, and rushed out of the parking lot. As soon as they entered the highway, Carvalho told his early twenty-something colleague to turn off the siren. It was far more irritating to hear it inside a police car than on the highway from many cars away.

After a few minutes of silence, Oliveira started speaking to Giles, clearly wanting to practice his English. "So, senhor Roberts, where is your niece from in the US?"

Ignoring the mistake of being called 'senhor Roberts', Giles wanted to avoid their conversation. He had an aversion to being with the police, even in the most innocuous of occasions. But his inborn politeness required him to answer. "She's from Philadelphia. Where did you learn to speak such good English?"

"Good English? Do you really think so? I learned it since primary school, as we all have. But I've taken it more seriously than most. I watch all the US police detective series on TV. Subtitles on my favorite YouTube music videos are a great help. I can't afford to take proper English classes. But I make up for it in any other way I can. I've tried to transfer to where the tourists are, like downtown Cascais, but so far, no luck.

"Philadelphia, huh? I really hope to meet her one day. I mean today. I love all things from the US: their music, Hollywood, fashion, their graphic art, their police detective novels. I'm reading one now about a young woman art forger in LA who's framed for murder by Russians and must go there to clear her name."

Giles interrupted him. "A young woman art forger, did you say? Look, Principal Agent Oliveira, this all sounds very interesting, but I'm not in the mood for conversation. I'm extremely stressed about my niece and can't think about anything else. So, if you don't mind, let's be quiet."

The disappointed driver replied, "Yes, sir, senhor Roberts. Whatever you say, sir." Oliveira, in his frustration, reached for the siren button again, but Carvalho slapped it away. "Just drive."

CHAPTER TWENTY-TWO

Gwendolyn was completely crushed by her failed attempt to escape. She was so close! It never occurred to her that there would be followers of George in that café bar. But of course, there would be. Why did she not just continue running until she was far away? Anger and frustration, in turn, engulfed her heart. Finally, exhaustion took over. She laid down on her thin straw mat, turning her eyes away from the constant light shining dully from a hole in the ceiling, covered by a metal grate nearly hidden behind old dusty cobwebs.

The emotional, mental, and finally the physical exhaustion took their toll. She slipped into a restless, uneasy sleep. Her dreams were incoherent, mostly quick images of horror: black shadows filled with the never-ending screams of the accursed. She twisted and turned to escape the depredations of the leering demons leaping out of the dark brandishing knives to cut a piece of her body off.

Gwendolyn found herself in a cave poorly lit with burning torches held by demons. She ran towards a brightly lit rocky room and away from her tormentors. They followed her, flying with their leathery bat wings, screeching in delight of the chase. The brilliantly illuminated room turned out to be a bonfire of the damned tied to stakes being burned alive.

After several more brief snatches of hellish scenes, she saw the gaping mouth of the cave. She ran out and at once entered an enormous field under a blood-red moon that pulsated like a heart. Below it, a massive burning lake swarmed with more of the damned gnashing their teeth and screaming in their pain. Terror filled her heart with dread, as there was nowhere to run. Suddenly, the ground gave way beneath her feet, and she fell into a deep cavernous black hole.

Falling as if someone pushed her off a high cliff, her hands desperately tried to grab anything, but only snatched empty air. A dank, moldy breeze swept around her as she plummeted for what seemed an eternity. Finally, she hit the stony floor in the cave where her dream had started.

She woke up on the stone floor with her straw mat covering her like a blanket. She must have rolled off the stone slab that served as her bed. Her dreams being so intense, she did not even wake up immediately when she landed on the floor, thinking that the hard slam was part of her nightmarish torture.

Did the ghost of Steven push her off in revenge for her treachery, hoping that she, too, would hit her head and end up with the same sightless stare from the very spot on the floor? But if he did, his attempt failed. A different fate awaited her at midnight.

The sun was already rising in the morning sky. Birds chirped. The sky was blue. It was turning into a wonderful day — a wonderful day to have her life snatched from her young heart. At midnight of that very day, when the cold, pale, silent moon at its fullest would be at its apex, George would rip out her heart with his black blade of obsidian.

Gwendolyn rose from the cold floor and walked to her cell's sole window. She forced the terrible memories of her dream from her mind. But the numbness of her helplessness would not allow her to replace it with anything else. The windowsill was just above her nose. She pulled herself up. Resting on her forearms with her feet dangling, she could look out the window.

The windows had thick bars with no glass. Maybe one of the previous victims broke the glass to slit her wrists, and they removed the remaining glass, never repairing it. Weeds and grass hid the view of the fields from her. Yet she could gaze upon the boundless blue sky above.

A hard ruffian face filled the barred window of the cell door. "Hey, what are you doing? Get down from there!"

Gwendolyn turned and dropped to the floor. "Just looking out the window."

"Well, don't." The door opened. The other guard placed a paper plate on the floor with a half a loaf of bread and a plastic cup of water. "Your brunch has arrived. Time to eat."

They laughed as they slammed the cell door. She quickly grabbed the bread and devoured it. She was famished. She washed it down with the cup of water. At least her hunger and thirst were lessened. Her stomach stopped growling, giving her some temporary peace.

Ignoring the bullies' warning, she returned to her windowsill perch. Dangling her feet freely in the air gave a strange sense of comfort. Perhaps the thought that she would be soon released from the mortal world of woe and her feet would float high above to wherever her soul was bound to go gave her feverish mind something else to ponder.

Her dreary dreamy state was suddenly broken when a field mouse burst through the grass in front of her face. With a quick gasp, she dropped onto the rocky floor. She backed away and returned to her bed of stone. She was not afraid of field mice or even rats. It was simply the suddenness of it.

The little furry life dropped onto her cell floor and ran around the room, looking for somewhere to hide. But there was none. Why would it do that? Then the answer came. A cat appeared between the bars of the window. The calico stared with great interest at the scampering mouse below.

She calmly leaped down and slowly approached the panicked mouse. Gwendolyn wondered what she should do. Should she save the mouse? But how? It would probably bite her if she tried to pick it up. An even more important question was why? Nature was merely playing itself out as it has done every day since the earth's creation.

When she was a young girl, her family had a calico cat. Gwendolyn's mother named her Euterpe after the Greek Muse of Tragedy. The little furry visitor before her reminded her of her special childhood friend. Euterpe did the same with whatever caught the attention of her emerald eyes: birds, squirrels, mice. She would bring them back as gifts placed on the backdoor stoop. Once she had placed a rat as an offering, but it was cut cleanly in two as if a cleaver toting butcher chopped it in half. Euterpe at least had the aesthetic sense to place the two halves in their correct order.

Euterpe would follow her like a puppy following its master through the Pennsylvania forests, stretching far behind her house. Over time, Gwendolyn learned exactly where the boundaries of Euterpe's domain lay. If she crossed the invisible frontier, Euterpe simply would not continue a step further.

There were two neighborhood bully dogs then that had no sense of frontiers or even of personal boundaries. Though each was three times Euterpe's size, she always succeeded in chasing them away. Every time she gave them another scar on their faces to remind them of their folly. The reflections of her distant past drove the despair away. In the end, she had to side with the busy calico.

The cat towered over the cringing mouse; its little flanks heaving in panic. A paw of claws batted the mouse, which set it running into another corner. That caused immense feline delight. The cat pounced and tossed the squeaking mouse into the air. It landed and was motionless. The cat stared at it with intense concentration. The mouse was playing dead, but not fooling anyone. Another clawed bat sent the mouse scurrying again. This game continued for over five minutes before the cat lunged and sank her teeth into the unlucky mouse.

Gwendolyn watched the whole show with fascination. "Bravo, kitty! Bravo!" She spoke softly to the cat. It was only then that Calico, as she so named her without any thought, noticed her with the limp mouse tightly clenched in her mouth. They stared at each other for a minute until she effortlessly leapt up to the window and disappeared into the tall grass.

She marveled at what had just happened. It certainly distracted her from her own terrible situation. Were there any parallels? Was George the cat and she the mouse? He had caught her and was toying with her like Calico did with the mouse. But the similarity stopped there. Calico did what cats have done to mice since they climbed out of the primordial seas. The mouse would be her meal and maybe for her babies hiding somewhere nearby.

George was merely satisfying his criminally insane desire to please his imaginary mother goddess. There was nothing natural about serial murder. The craziest thing of all was how he managed to convince a large number of strangers to help him, to serve him as the grandmaster of his bloody cult.

Rage consumed her as she paced back and forth across the cell floor. Her blind anger reflected her utter hopelessness. This went on for about an hour until a meow from the window froze her in her tracks. Calico had returned.

Gwendolyn calmly advanced, speaking gently and kindly to her. With her arms held out, she was just below the cat. She offered the back of her hand to the furry face. Calico sniffed and then rubbed her face against Gwendolyn's hand. She petted her until Calico allowed the distressed young woman to pick her up and place her on her lap.

Calico stretched on her new human's lap and purred. Bastet, the ancient Egyptian Cat Goddess, sent at least a modest balm to help her in her time of despair. Gwendolyn's racing heart slowed as she pet the warm furry animal, who had taken a liking to her, enough to trust that her new-found human would not harm her.

Harming her was the furthest thing from her mind. The hours passed as she stared numbly at the sky through the small cell window. The sun was slowly but steadily sinking in the sky. There was no sign of Rui or Giles. They could never find her in that damp, moldy hole, anyway. What little hope she had faded as the afternoon light waned.

Outside the cell, she could hear the devotees of that horrid goddess of death preparing the scene of her doom. They were thoroughly sweeping, washing, and cleaning. They replaced all the candles with new ones. George stood on a ladder and lovingly dusted his mother goddess. He did the same for the sacks of shrunken heads, removing cobwebs with the remains of flies uneaten by their eight-legged captors who had since moved on.

He inspected the black obsidian knife that his Mexican chapter of the goddess gave him. It was ready for its important task. The four colorful festive silk ribbons were prepared to tie the victim's four limbs to the corners of the waiting altar, a different color for each direction, according to Chinese tradition: north/black, south/red, east/bluish green, and west/white. The altar was never washed, as George preferred it to remain bathed in the blood of his sacrifices. The goddess had told him she liked to be reminded in this way of his special service to her.

He whistled as he worked, despite his swollen eye. It would be an incredibly significant night soon. The sunset was filling the sky with its beautiful hues. Midnight was approaching. George could see the goddess's lurid grimacing mouth form into a smile. She would soon be proud of her son. All would be right in the world again.

Gwendolyn cringed as she heard all the busy preparations and the bizarre, jolly whistling. She held Calico tightly against her breast. For her part, she licked Gwendolyn's ears, purring all the time. The little animal sensed her anxiety. Knowing that her task was to calm the madly beating heart of her new friend, she would not leave Gwendolyn's lap.

The sun had set, and the moon was rising. It was night already. No one was coming to save her. Gwendolyn resolved that her end was near. She would face it with dignity, but not calmly. She still had one trick literally up her sleeve: the spring-loaded knife strapped to her inner forearm. Assuming they would tie her down by her hands and feet, she pushed the knife higher up her arm, making it more difficult to notice.

She had no idea just yet how and when she would use it but use it she would. She had to take out George, if not to save herself, at least to save future redheaded victims from the same horrid fate. It was the sole thought consuming her mind. She was so homed in on that deed that she became calm again. It was no time for panicking.

Suddenly, a trumpet blasted. The cell door opened, and six men rushed in, two of them pointing pistols at her head. At the sound of the door opening, Calico leaped off her lap and hid behind the door.

George's thugs all wore the same white robes they had given Gwendolyn. Instead of the expected screaming, crying, begging, or desperate fighting that the other victims gave, she calmly rose and stretched out her arms. Surprised at how willing and cooperative the latest victim was, they stood still for a moment.

Soon they recovered, and each one tied a silk ribbon to her wrists and ankles. They did not have to struggle with her and roughly manhandle her to the altar. She stood in their center, faced the door, and serenely walked out to her impending doom, with the ribbons trailing behind her.

CHAPTER TWENTY-THREE

During the hour it took to arrive, all Giles could do was look out the window without noticing a thing. His mind was in turmoil, careening between hope and fear. Apparently, they found George's lair. But was she even there? If so, was she still alive? The prepared but empty grave implied she was. Would they arrive in time? Would George kill her before his eyes as soon as they burst through the door? Giles thought it was all too much for a simple art dealer.

It was already dusk when Oliveira pulled off the highway. Two minutes later, four police cars with sixteen policemen standing in small groups came into view. He found a space and parked the car. Everyone got out.

A tall man in his early fifties approached with a military air, "Good evening. I'm Superintendent (Captain) Jorge Queiróz. And you must be Commissioner Carvalho? I saw those photos you forwarded me. Very interesting, very interesting indeed. This might be something big. As you can see, I brought most of my precinct with me. We'll get to the bottom of this." He offered his hand to the one wearing the three stars of the commissioner insignia.

"Yes, sir, I'm him. This here is Principal Agent Oliveira and these two are the ones who identified the place. This one, Rui Silveira, is the pilot of the plane and a friend of the young woman in question. This is her uncle Roberts who took the photos. He's English and doesn't speak Portuguese."

Superintendent Queiróz shook hands in the reverse order of the introduction. "Mr. Roberts, I'm so sorry for what you are going through. Rest assured, if your niece is there, we will find and rescue her. Ah, you look surprised. I was in our military and served as part of the UN peacekeeping force in the former Yugoslavia back in the nineties. The language of communication was English."

"I'm very glad to meet you, Superintendent. You can just call me Robert. You have my utmost confidence that you'll end this terrible thing as soon as possible."

"Indeed, we will. We'll wait until after dark before arriving there. We must take them by surprise. All those men I saw cutting weeds in the field tell me that this will not be a simple operation. They probably are armed, too. Now, if you'll excuse me, I want to discuss our plan with Commissioner Carvalho."

Those two walked out of earshot, leaving Oliveira, Rui, and Giles staring after them in silence. The other policemen were standing around smoking and speaking excitedly. This probably would be the largest operation ever conducted by their regional precinct since the communist-hunting days of Salazar seventy years before. Finally, they would have something to tell their children for many decades to come.

As the daylight waned, Oliveira regained his self-confidence. "Senhor Mr. Roberts, sir, my responsibility is to protect you and be your interpreter while we rescue your niece. And of course, Senhor Silveira here. Well, except for the interpreting part."

"Hmm, that's a relief, I guess," was all Giles could reply. He left them and wandered absently around the periphery of the parked cars, impatiently waiting for the moon to rise and the operation to start. Having an ex-military man in charge gave him more confidence. He had doubts about Commissioner Carvalho's ability to pull it off. Nonetheless, he could not hide the anxiety on his face.

Rui caught up with him. They walked together in silence. Finally, he spoke, "Robert, I know this is very difficult for you. But don't worry. The police are taking this very seriously, as you can see by all these men gathered here. Superintendent Queiróz strikes me as a man of ability who can pull this off.

"I also am confident that if I can have the chance to just talk to George, I can convince him to let her go. I'll promise him anything, to forgive everything, even to return to the UK with him just as in the old times." Rui's voice rose as the mere thought gave him much anguish.

"Thank you for that, Rui. Unfortunately for him, if he is indeed the serial killer of redheaded women, the police will not allow him to simply go. He'd know that. He would probably become desperate when we show up. No, I must put my trust in the superintendent. God, I'd like to know what their plan is! Is it logical? Will it work?"

Rui had nothing to say. They found a large rock and sat down together. He looked at his watch and estimated they had to wait for another hour before it was truly dark enough. Rather than sit in gloomy silence the whole time, he started to speak.

"You know, Robert, I have been in similar situations like this before. I attended a boarding school in England from when I was fourteen until I graduated at the age of eighteen. Later I went to a university in Scotland to study naval design. But I did not go to university right after secondary school. Oh no, not at all. I was drafted to do my Portuguese military service.

"In those days, we were deep over our heads fighting terrible wars to maintain our African colonies. All young men had to serve four years with a minimum of two of them fighting in Africa. Like many others at the time, I could have stayed in the UK and ignored it altogether, as hundreds of thousands of my fellow young Portuguese men did. But by doing so, I could never return to Portugal. My family and I just had too much here for me to cut ties, including my home in Estoril and cork plantations in Alentejo. It would have been a grand shame and crisis for my family. So, I returned to do what had to be done.

"Luckily, I had learned to fly small planes while I was in boarding school. Fortunately, our military understood there was value to that. So, I flew small reconnaissance planes in northern Mozambique. I didn't have to slog it out in the jungles and the bushland like all the other poor grunts. Though I was occasionally shot at from the ground, nothing serious happened. I could have hot meals and sleep in a cot off the ground every day after I returned to the well-protected airfield.

"But one morning, unusual news came in on the airfield radio. A unit of guerillas had taken the mayor hostage in one of the smaller towns still loyal to us in our sector. We had to do something at once. There was no time to organize a rescue with a ground operation. It was simply too far to reach him. I was tasked with flying a team of five commandos there in my small plane. I could land on most any flat field. The harvest season had already come to an end. So, there were many fields to land close to our target.

"After I landed at a field as close as I could get to the mayor's house, I expected to stay with my plane while they did what they had to do. But oh no. I was ordered to take my rifle that I kept stored in the hold of the plane and help them secure the hostage. I was shocked, as I had never fired my rifle in anger. But there is no time to be shocked for long in a combat situation. So, I followed them and did what they did: crouched, crawled, ran, etc.

"We entered the ground floor by hopping through open windows. We quietly searched every room on the floor. Our commando captain and his lieutenant silently took out the two guerrillas we found there. I had never seen anyone killed before, not even a dead person by natural causes. I nearly lost it. One of the younger commandos grabbed me by the throat and covered my mouth. I quickly got it together again.

"The only other direction was up. So, we quietly crept up the stairs. We searched the other rooms, taking out two more guerrillas as before. Finally, the only room left was the mayor's study and office. The door was locked. One of my comrades swiftly took out a crowbar and forced the flimsy wooden door open. We burst in and opened fire on the guerrillas lounging in the easy chairs. I fired in their general direction, knocking one down. Later, I found out that I killed him. Still haven't gotten over that.

"The guerrilla captain held the mayor close with a pistol pressed tightly against his temple. A rescued but dead mayor would still be a victory for the guerillas. Our captain pointed his rifle at the head of the guerrilla leader. They shouted at each other, both threatening to shoot first. Both considering the results if they did. One would be a dead mayor and the other a victorious but dead guerrilla. Probably both would happen. What would that mean in the end?

"I was so nervous, completely out of my depth. My hands were shaking like leaves in the breeze. I remember I took my finger off the trigger, afraid that I would shoot someone by accident. Suddenly, I dropped my rifle, and it fired when it hit the floor. No one was hit, but it caused a distraction. The guerrilla was startled and looked at me. That's when our captain shot him dead, saving the mayor.

"I was a hero to our commandos. I would later receive a medal for that, though the details were changed in the report. I felt ashamed, really. While we were still at the mayor's house, we were attacked by the remaining guerillas outside. I could see through the windows that there were a few trying to damage the plane. That really infuriated me, as she was my baby. I told the commandos to cover me as I had to save our plane, or we would never get out of there. They did, and I ran to the plane screaming like one possessed by demons, firing my rifle at them from my hip.

"I didn't hit anyone, but they got the message and fled. The others saw their mates running away. They decided it was time to give up and melt back into the bushland. This part went into a separate report, and I received another commendation. That one I deserved, though I acted without thinking about it."

"Interesting, Rui, but what's your point?"

"My point is… well, it's that I've been in a hostage rescue situation before and with proper leadership as we have here, I don't think you need to worry about anything."

"Hm, if you say so. OK, so what happened after all that? What happened after Africa? Did you serve your other two years somewhere else?"

"I resumed flying simple reconnaissance missions. Everyone treated me with the utmost respect. Eventually, they sent me to do training on jet fighters back here in Portugal. But I was a confused boy then. I thought I would enjoy playing for the other team."

"The other team?"

"Yeah, you know, playing on the all-boys team."

"That's what I thought you meant."

"OK, I thought I was gay. An officer seduced me, and we were caught. Militaries frown on this kind of thing. They could have dishonorably discharged me, which would have been a great shame for my family and me for life. Except for my 'bravery under fire' commendations in Mozambique, they would have. But with those two attached to my file, they decided to simply let me go for 'psychological' reasons. I immediately returned to the UK to continue my studies; two years older and many more years wiser."

"Why do militaries discriminate so against gays? They can be as brave and 'manly' as anyone else."

"I suppose it's because it would be bad for morale, or it would be too much of a distraction. I don't know."

"Yet many militaries have women in combat positions like the US and Israel, among others. I'd think mixing young women and men close together in their late teens would be very distracting to everybody."

"I've no answer. Maybe the generals think gays aren't manly enough, but young women are. In any case, that's my story." Suddenly, Rui pointed to the sky. "Look, we can see the moon through the clouds. We must be almost ready to go."

On cue, Oliveira ran up to announce it was time. They all were getting into their respective cars. Giles' heart leapt as he closed his car door. Finally! The waiting was over.

The car engines were idling. A car left while the remaining cars waited. "What are we waiting for?" Giles nearly shouted.

Oliveira translated Carvalho's explanation. "There is a café bar between here and there. That car will serve as a scout. They'll make sure no one there will call and warn our target that we are arriving. No one could miss six police cars driving down this narrow country lane. Once we're all clear. It should only take about fifteen or twenty minutes to get there."

"Hmm, OK, that makes sense. Seems like Queiróz knows what he's doing."

Indeed, the scout car parked in front of the very same café bar that Gwendolyn had visited the night before. The four occupants of the car entered, causing quite a stir. The owner rushed over and asked what was the matter? Were they off duty and wanted something to drink?

No, they were merely doing a police exercise, the senior officer replied. He asked that everyone leave their cellphones in their pockets and keep their hands on the table. They could carry on drinking or playing cards in the meantime. No one was allowed to leave or even go to the restroom. He apologized for any inconvenience.

He left two junior officers there to keep an eye on things. He and the other one left, leaving the customers murmuring to themselves. Once outside, he called Queiróz, informing him everything was under control, and it was safe to continue.

Queiróz' car led the others with Carvalho's behind him. They drove slowly with the headlights off. The patchy moonlight was all that lit the way. Giles was nearly beside himself impatiently wishing the car ahead of theirs to go faster. The moon cast weak foreboding shadows of the dark farmhouses they passed. This gloom fueled his despair even more. His mind continued repeating the word: *Gwendolyn, we're on our way. Stay safe, dear friend. We're almost there!*

Though it seemed to Giles they were merely inching along, the ruined farmhouse emerged behind the crumbling wall within the twenty minutes Oliveira had said. They parked the cars blocking the road to prevent any possible escape by a car full of cultists making a mad dash for it. The officers excitedly opened the car trunks. They put on helmets, flak jackets, and various other equipment. Everyone armed themselves with automatic rifles.

The only escape was on foot, but no one was leaving that walled ruin. Queiróz sent three officers to surround the outside of the walls in case someone climbed over and tried to make a run for it. The rest gathered around the only functioning gate. Two others held the chain so it would not clang against the iron gate when they severed it. Others sprayed lubricant on the hinges. One of them walked up with bolt cutters and quickly snapped off the chain. The gate opened silently.

Queiróz sent another one to approach the only source of light visible at the far end of the house, which was otherwise as dark and silent as a tomb. The specialist crept over and laid low beside the small window just above ground level. He pulled out a miniature telescope that he could bend to see around corners. He maneuvered it to slightly beyond the window frame and peered through.

His voice whispered through Queiróz' earpiece. "Sir, I confirm that a young woman is sitting in what appears to be a locked cell. She's a redhead. Wait! Six men have just entered. Two of them are armed with side arms. The others are tying her wrists and ankles with colored ribbons… Now they're escorting her out." Queiróz replied, "OK, you stay there and guard that side against anyone trying to escape. The rest of you take your positions. Let's move out."

He motioned to Rui and Giles not to make a sound and to stay by the gate with Oliveira. Two others quickly went to the other two unguarded sides of the house and crouched against the stone walls. Once they were in position, the remaining nine clustered around the heavy wooden door that led to the basement, the only functioning door in the whole ruin.

Carvalho held his nose as he pointed to the already rotting pile of flesh that was all that remained of the errant Steven, his well-scraped skeleton still secured to the stone pillar a few paces from the door. Queiróz and the others pulled their kerchiefs up to cover their mouths and noses. They could still smell the sickly-sweet stench of putrid flesh, but it was better than nothing. One of them disappeared around the corner of the farmhouse to vomit.

Another officer put on his thick gloves and prepared the enforcer, a one-man battering ram used to break door locks with three tons of impact force. Three others readied concussion grenades to throw in after the door was broken down. The vomiting one returned, wiping his mouth clean and picked up his hastily dropped rifle. His boss was not impressed.

Once Queiróz was satisfied everyone was ready and in place, he whispered to the one holding the enforcer, "OK, let's knock on the door and see if anyone's home."

CHAPTER TWENTY-FOUR

Gwendolyn walked hesitantly to the opened cell door. The moaning of thirty mouths suddenly ceased when they saw her appear. She, too, stopped. Everyone was enrobed in white, except for George standing behind the stone altar and in front of the terrible statue of the bloodthirsty goddess. He wore a black robe with a large medallion of a scallop shell swaying from his neck like the one Venus had risen on from the sea.

The center of the room was dark where the adherents were kneeling. They were only visible from the light of the hundreds of candles from the surrounding walls. Two brass incense burners stood   as tall as a person on either end of the altar. The incense smelled like opium. The competing scents assailing her, making her squeamish.

She sensed all eyes were staring at her, even the sewn eyes of all the shrunken heads of the previous victims trapped in the mesh sacks were staring at her. George smiled and beckoned for her to approach.

"Come here, my child. It's time for you to meet your destiny. Come, come, don't be shy."

Gwendolyn had no choice but to walk as slowly as she could despite the pushes from behind. She wanted to get as close to him as necessary to stick her knife in his jugular vein. She could not risk someone finding her knife if they had to carry her there. Approaching the dreadful stone block, she trembled, not sure what to do or even how to do it. She was waiting for her moment, but those moments were running out.

As she considered simply running and pouncing on him before anyone could react, four sets of hands grabbed tightly the ribbons tied to her ankles and wrists. She was not running anywhere. They nudged her to the waiting stone slab. Slowly, she lifted herself up and onto the cold seat of death. She was spread out as each ribbon was tied securely to an iron ring hanging just below each corner of the altar with her right-side facing George. Her escorts stepped away.

George stood above her. "Oh, my sweet lamb, I'm so glad to see that you are willingly embracing your role in this very special event. In fact, I'm so pleased that I will honor my promise to you. I'll make this as quick and painless as I can. Please forgive me if you feel a twinge or two. Afterall, I'm no surgeon. But I promise I'll try my best.

"Allow me to explain. The ritual is rather simple and short. After our majestic goddess blesses the blade, I will quickly cut your heart out of your chest. While it still weakly beats, your brain may have enough blood and consciousness to see it and even understand what it means for a brief second. After that, all will be darkness, until your sisters greet you on the other side of the vale. They will show you how to pay homage to the Great Mother. Her radiance will light the way, as the sunrise reveals the secrets of the night."

He smiled serenely as he raised the obsidian blade between is palms. Turning to the towering statue behind him, he began to chant in High Church Latin, beseeching the goddess to bless the tool that would deliver her another servant. During these fifteen minutes of chanting, she struggled to sever the ribbon holding her right hand. She was becoming desperate, not wanting to cut her own veins and bleed out to no effect. She had to rid the world of this monster.

George turned and spoke to her as a father would to a young child. "Now, my dear, the time has come for your soul to join our Goddess Mother and serve her for all eternity. It was a bit of a rough ride getting here, but you managed to arrive in the end. I thank you for that. The goddess thanks you and has communicated to me that she is eager to meet you in person. I've told her so much about you."

Gwendolyn started to shout a curse at him, but he pressed his fingers tightly against her mouth. "No, my child, it is not the time for words. You will speak your next words to your goddess and mistress when you meet her. I must say, I'm jealous. I would love to join her, but she only accepts young women with your special mark, your red hair. I'm bound to serve her by sending her faithful servants. The moon is full and high above us. It is time now. Goodbye."

The evil black blade rose above her. Her breath choked in her throat. Horror filled her mind and shut off her peripheral vision and hearing. Her focus centered on that blade above her. Just as George was set to plunge his knife into her chest and cut out her heart, she suddenly felt a light weight on her breasts.

Calico had understood her new friend was in danger and had come out of hiding. She leapt on Gwendolyn's chest, arched her back, and hissed at George. George, utterly surprised, stepped back.

What was this, a demon come to protect the spawn of his master? George regained his composure and swiftly brought his knife down, sending Bastet's representative flying off the altar. He raised his blade again.

Thanks to Calico's intervention, Gwendolyn had the time to finally sever the ribbon she was struggling with. She made a fist and pulled her hand as far back as she could, before ramming her knife into George's scrotal sac. She twisted it sharply. He dropped the black blade and fell to his knees. She quickly rolled over to cut free her left hand, avoiding the falling glass blade, which shattered into tiny pieces as it hit the stone altar.

She sat up and freed her legs. George struggled to breathe as he held his groin. All Gwendolyn could see was red rage. She grabbed his hair and lifted his head. He looked at her with terror-filled eyes.

"You are the evil one who must be destroyed! You will do no more harm! Ever! I will now send you to serve your devil mistress." Gwendolyn screamed as she severed George's head from his neck. She screamed like a banshee. Blood spurted everywhere. She stood, holding his decapitated head, and faced the shocked men. Their faces were frozen in horror, speechless. Their master's still open eyes stared at them blankly.

"You stupid blind bastards! See? This was your master! But I! I am the goddess before you and I have claimed what is mine. You shall bow down and worship me. On your faces! Now!"

Gwendolyn shook as she stood on the altar high above them. She swung George's head like an incense censer at a high church mass. She brandished her knife. All the recent thugs at once fell prone with their faces on the floor crying like babes who lost their security blanket.

Just then, a tremendous bang smashed the door and burst it open. Superintendent Queirós was shocked to find Gwendolyn screaming with a severed head in her hand and all the men on the floor flat on their faces. He immediately stopped his colleagues from throwing in the concussion grenades. He faced the gate and called over to Rui and Giles. "It's done. She's safe. You can come over now."

They ran into the basement temple, while the police arrested the broken men, now just shells of themselves. Their world had just been shattered into tiny pieces. She was carrying on without change, still shrieking, shaking his head, and brandishing her knife. Giles approached her slowly with his arms extended.

"Come, Gwendolyn, come down, my friend. It's over. It's all over. Let me help you."

She could neither hear nor see anything around her. Everything was a dark shade of bloody crimson red. She swung at Giles' outstretched arms, nearly cutting off his hand. He swiftly stepped back. Rui tried to speak to her, but to the same effect.

It was all too much for the gentle nature of Giles. He kneeled before her and sobbed, "Gwendolyn! It's me! Don't you remember? My dearest, please! It's finished. You won. George is gone. Please, my dearest, dearest Gwendolyn, please come down from there." His voice broke into sobs.

She suddenly stopped swinging her weapon and the villain's head. "What's this? Why aren't you on the floor like the rest of them? Who are you? You look familiar. Wait a minute. Is that really you? You came! You came to save me! Oh, I knew you would find me! I just knew you would!"

She turned and threw the head at the terrible statue. It left a bloody stain where it hit before falling to the floor with a thud. "Rui? You came, too? You were always a kind friend to me. Thank you. Now, will you two kindly give me your hands so I can get off this horrible thing?"

They helped her off the altar. They had to support her as she tried to walk to the open door and freedom. They passed an officer as he called out to Queirós, "Hey, Superintendent! I found a wounded cat here. It's been cut badly. What do you want me to do with it?"

Gwendolyn yelled, "Calico! That's my cat! Please take care of her and bring her to me as soon as you can. She saved my life, the poor dear."

"Well, there's your answer, Corporal. Wrap her in a blanket and place her in your car. Take her to the closest pet hospital. As for our heroine, how's she doing? I have never seen anyone manage to pacify thirty-some men as she did."

"She's very weak and probably in serious shock. She can hardly walk." They exited the stuffy basement into the cool, clear night air, helping her up the steps to the outside. Her robe dripped wet with blood. She glanced over at Steven's imperfectly cleaned skeleton attached to the pillar close to the door. She let out another screeching scream and collapsed to the ground. She hyperventilated for a few moments before fainting completely away. George still had managed to strike her, even after death.

Giles yelled to Queirós, "Superintendent! We need to get her to the hospital, right now!"

"I'll call for a helicopter to take her to the nearest emergency room. Hey, you two! Help these two gentlemen carry her to one of our cars. Wrap her in blankets and lay her in the back seat. Get her off the cold, damp ground and away from whatever that terrible thing is."

Giles was completely beside himself. There was nothing Rui could say to calm him. After they placed her carefully in the police car, Giles shouted to Queirós, who was in the middle of several officers reporting to him with great animation. "Superintendent! How long until the helicopter gets here?"

"In about thirty minutes."

"Thirty minutes! Why so long?"

"The closest one that is ready to be airborne is in Cascais. Luckily, we don't get many cases such as this in Portugal." Sensing Giles needed something to take his fevered mind off Gwendolyn's state, he continued, "Hey, we found something you might be very interested in seeing. Both of you, come with me. Oliveira can stay and keep an eye on her."

He led them back inside. The followers were lined up against the wall, too distraught to think of resisting or escaping. Queirós whistled as he pointed to the shrunken heads hanging from the rafters.

He stared at the grotesque idol. "Why the hell is that ugly statue grimacing like that?"

Rui answered, "That, I'm afraid, is George's personal Mother Goddess, whom he made into a worldwide cult. When you're ready for a full report, I can tell you all about it."

"Worldwide cult, did you say? Well then, you'll find this interesting." He ushered them into George's bedroom and study.

"You notice all those boxes on the shelves? Each box has a notebook, personal effects, and a lock of each victim's hair. He documented every murder he did in full detail. How he did it. Where he found her. Her name and nationality. Everything. These records cover each country he was active in. This must have been his headquarters or whatever you call this center of murder, a lair, perhaps. And gentlemen, so far, we've found ninety-seven individually named boxes.

"Behind this bookcase is a hidden passage. No idea where it leads, but we'll find out. Over here is some kind of kitchen, but not one for cooking any meal that I ever saw. What the hell was he doing here?"

"That, Superintendent, I believe, is where he shrunk the heads of his victims. The ones which are hanging in those sacks out there."

"Really? I'd never have guessed. What a sick bastard! What on earth was he thinking? Now over here on his desk we found files with records and names of all his other temples, as he calls them, and his active followers. Interpol will be very busy very soon rounding up these sickos. His diaries will reveal a lot, too."

He patted Commissioner Carvalho on the back. "Great job, Commissioner, for not brushing this off as merely a prank call. You have shown excellent insight and judgment. I'll make sure my report makes clear your important role in this. Hm? I believe I hear a helicopter approaching. Let's go give whatever help we can to the poor young woman."

By the time they left behind the temple of terror, the helicopter had landed on the recently cleared field. The medics rushed to where Oliveira was waving. They put her on a stretcher and carried her quickly to the helicopter. As they were giving Gwendolyn their first responder care, Queirós motioned for them to get in, too.

"You two can go with her. She'll need familiar faces when she wakes up. The officers who took the cat to her hospital called me a little while ago. Tell her that her cat will recover in a week or so. She might hobble and not have any babies, but she'll live. That bit of news should help her, too.

"I'll be in touch and will follow up with the hospital. Here's my card if you need anything. At least, let me know where to send the cat. Senhor Robert, I may need to contact you later for any details you can provide. I'll contact you at your hotel. As for you, Senhor Silveira, you can certainly expect a visit from me very soon. Glancing at the last few entries in his most recent diary, I noticed your name came up quite a lot, mostly in anger. Don't plan on leaving on a trip any time in the near future."

The first responders finished fussing over her, safely securing her in place. They gave a thumbs up to Queiróz. Giles and Rui climbed in, taking their seats where the responders indicated.

"OK, everything is ready. Take care of that young woman. It's incredible what she's been through. Horrible really. Strap in and good luck."

CHAPTER TWENTY-FIVE

As soon as the helicopter landed, Gwendolyn was whisked off to the emergency room. Giles and Rui followed as far as they could but were left pacing outside in the waiting room. It was after 0200 when the doctor came out to report.

"Gentlemen, hello, I'm Doctor Ferreira. That young lady took quite a shock. The police Superintendent Queirós described to me what she went through. All I can say is wow! You're probably wondering how she's doing. Well, she's sedated, and her vital signs are stable."

Giles nearly shouted, "That's it? That's all you can tell us? Will she live?"

Rui patted him on the back. "Let's let the good doctor continue."

The good doctor continued, "She's young and her heart's strong. She should pull through fine. The first twenty-four hours will be crucial. We'll just have to wait and see after she wakes up. I understand you are very distraught. You can stay with her through the night and tomorrow, too, if you want. Superintendent Queirós requested that she be put in a private room.

"Nurse Tavares here will take you there. We will be monitoring her at all times. So, don't worry. We'll take excellent care of her. That's about all I can report for the moment. So, if there are no more questions, I need to return to the emergency department. Good evening, gentlemen."

Rui pulled Giles back, as he wanted to follow the doctor with more questions. "Robert, there's nothing more he can tell us or even do. Let's go with Nurse Tavares to see our heroine. Maybe she's awake already."

Giles reluctantly gave way. They followed the nurse through endless corridors and up several floors before she stopped in front of a room. She opened the door, revealing Gwendolyn unconscious in a hospital bed with an IV suspended above her. Several electronic monitoring devices beeped quietly next to her, each connected to her in different ways.

Giles rushed over and held her hand. Rui motioned to the nurse that she could leave. Tears came to Giles' eyes seeing her in such a state. Her experience this time was worse than what she suffered in Russia during a previous art project of theirs.

Giles whispered in her ear, "I'm so sorry, dear Gwendolyn, to have put you through this. Who would have thought such a horrible thing could happen in peaceful Portugal? But don't you worry. I'm right here and will not leave your side until you're well again. Sleep now. But tomorrow please wake up and tell me you're fine. Please, my dear, please." His tears wetted the side of her face.

After giving him a moment to express his grief, Rui put his arm on Giles' shoulder. "There's a sofa here. We can take shifts sleeping and watching her. You can sleep first."

"Sleep? Impossible! ... OK, you're right. I am exhausted. Wake me in three hours. That'll be about 0530. You need your sleep, too."

Rui agreed and set his cellphone's alarm. He stared intensely at Gwendolyn, occasionally gazing at the gently beeping green waves the monitors made on their small screens. Sleep slowly descended on him. He nodded off until the vibration of his cellphone alarm in his pants pocket woke him. He stood up and stretched.

Silently, Rui gave Giles a gentle pat on the shoulder and nodded. It was his turn to fret about Gwendolyn. Rui took his place on the sofa and fell into a fitful sleep. He awoke two hours later when another nurse entered the room to check on their patient. She made a few adjustments and whispered, "Everything looks fine. Don't worry."

Giles whispered after her, "Don't worry? I've never been more worried in my life."

Rui shook his head and laid back down. Giles did not set his alarm to allow Rui to sleep longer. Giles felt like he was on the edge of a mental breakdown himself. Despite his best efforts not to, he nodded off on the relatively comfortable padded chair.

It was nearly noon when the full light of the midday sun was leaking through the closed blinds. The nurse returned, awakening them both. Rui stood up from the sofa, yawned, and stretched. Giles awoke with a start.

The nurse repeated her checking and adjusting of all the apparatus connected to the still sleeping Gwendolyn. "Oh, I see you two are awake now. It was a late and apparently terrible time last night. Would you like something to eat? Our sleeping patient clearly is not interested in eating. I'll bring something for you as soon as I'm finished here. Shall I open the blinds?"

Rui gave her a nod. Suddenly, the room was bathed in light. The Atlantic Ocean was clearly visible from the window. The bright sun shining in the blue skies and on the azul ocean dazzled their eyes. They ate the surprisingly good lunch the nurse brought. Later, they took advantage of the private bath to shower and try to recover themselves. They both decided not to use the disposable paper underwear on offer.

As for Gwendolyn, they washed off the blood that covered her the best they could in the emergency room, where they cut off the ripped and blood-soaked rag that was her ritual robe and replaced it with a crisply clean hospital gown. Though she breathed calmly, her face and hair were a mess. She sorely needed a proper shower.

Late that afternoon, they snapped to attention when they heard her say weakly, "Where am I? Have I died and gone to heaven again?"

They rushed to her side, but she had already fallen asleep again. Rui motioned to him to let her sleep. Giles whispered excitedly, "Ah, look! She's no longer unconscious. She's asleep, but at least she's conscious. That's progress. Don't you think?"

It was early evening when Gwendolyn stirred and mistakenly pressed the emergency buzzer that was close beside her. Two nurses rushed in and fussed over her, making sure everything was alright. She tried to sit up. "Hey, hey, let go of me! Who are you? Where am I? Where are my friends? Where's my cat?" She fell back onto her pillow, exhausted from the effort.

Her two friends dashed over, each holding a weak hand. Giles nearly cried with joy. "Here we are, Gwendolyn. We're right here. We never left your side the whole time. Are you better?"

A nurse raised her bed to a forty-five-degree angle. The sedative had not completely worn off. She replied weakly. "Better? Oh, I've seen better days. You won't believe the nightmares I've had. The horrors!"

Giles replied, "I'm sure I can believe them. But they are all over now. You just need to rest, and you'll recover very quickly."

"Seems I remember I have a cat... Where's my Calico?"

"Calico? Ah, she's recovering herself at her own hospital. Her doctor assures us she'll be fine in about a week. But let's concentrate on you for now."

"So, I do have a cat? I don't remember having one before. As for me? What's there to concentrate on me?" Her words trailed off as she fell asleep once more.

A doctor had since entered the room. "She'll be fine by tomorrow. Even so, we'll keep her here for a few days to monitor her progress. We have rooms available if you want to spend the night here. The shop downstairs sells things like underwear, socks, toiletries, etc. if you need things like that.

"But I must advise you that though her heart and body are strong, she may need psychiatric help after she recovers physically. In any case, she'll need some time of peace and quiet without even the remotest possibility of stress. We'll just have to see and hope for the best. Let the nurses know if you need anything else." He bowed slightly and left.

Rui and Giles were left staring at each other, not knowing how to process the last part of the doctor's summary. Finally, Rui suggested, "I don't know about you, but I think I'll make use of the rooms and try to get a better night's sleep. It's taken a huge toll on you and me both."

Giles agreed. "Fine. But I want to make a quick visit to pick up a few things at the hospital store before doing that. My socks and underwear are ready to retire."

"Good idea. Let's go."

By the end of the next day, she was sitting up and watching the news on the TV attached to the wall in front of her. Giles and Rui were always with her. She spoke very little and seemed depressed.

The news repeated Queirós interview regarding his ending the rampaging serial killer internationally known as the Scarlet Head Cutter for the tenth time that day. The English closed captions allowed Giles and Gwendolyn to understand the Portuguese.

Rui whispered to Giles that he hoped that Commissioner Carvalho would get some of the fame.

"So, Superintendent Queirós, what more can you say about this gruesome find in our own backyard?"

"Well, gruesome it is. I'll not go into details on public television, but I can tell you that I've never seen anything like it, even during wartime and certainly never in the modern history of our country. May it never happen again."

"What can you tell us about the perpetrator? Was he Portuguese?"

"I can't say much currently until the investigation is complete, both here and in the other countries where he committed his crimes. I can at least say he was not a Portuguese national."

"How many murders was he responsible for?"

"Again, I cannot say for sure until all the investigations are completed in the various countries in which he operated."

"How about in Portugal? We can see the outlines of graves here in the field."

"Yet again, we're not sure. But as you can see for yourself, there are twenty-three what appear to be graves right over there. There's another new one under that oak tree where the old family cemetery is. Until we exhume and investigate the remains, we can't give any definite answer to that question either."

"Does Superintendent Queirós have any idea why the victims were all young redheaded women?"

"We don't have any definitive answer to this either. However, it appears that the perpetrator kept all his worldwide records of every murder and his victims here. It will take time to study these records and piece together all the evidence. As of now, that's still a mystery."

"Superintendent, there are rumors that all of this was part of some strange cult. Can you share any insight into this?"

"I'm no specialist in that area. There certainly were many strange things surrounding these serial murders. But I'm not at liberty to say just yet."

"According to the neighbors, they saw two full medium-sized police buses taking many perpetrators into custody. How many were there and were there any Portuguese among them?"

"We have thirty-two suspects in custody. All I'm able to say is that only a few were Portuguese."

"Superintendent, how did you even find this place serving as the center of these terrible crimes?"

"Ah, that at least is an answer I can give. Let me call over the one who can answer that best. Hey, Commissioner Carvalho! Come over here!"

"Commissioner, the reporter would like to know how we found this place. I mean, how you found this place. This man is the real hero here. He had the power to dismiss it, but he didn't. Tell them how you did it. Excuse me, I need to go back to the investigation inside. Commissioner Carvalho can answer your questions." He patted Carvalho on his shoulder and made a quick exit from the unpleasant interview, something he never liked doing.

"Commissioner, Superintendent Queirós told us you can shed some light on how you discovered this place?"

"I'm so glad you asked." Carvalho straightened as tall as he could and smiled. "Well, it all started when a concerned citizen called regarding a missing person, a personal woman friend of his. I could have dismissed it as we receive calls about missing persons all the time, usually concerning lovers suddenly breaking up and the like. But something about this call was different. I decided to take it seriously. So, I asked him…"

Rui smiled and nodded at Giles. The interview continued for another ten minutes. Gwendolyn did not recognize anything that had any connection to her. She could not really follow the conversation, as the words of the subtitles were all running together.

Later, at the first scene of some different horror or another that was happening somewhere else in the world that day, Gwendolyn screamed, causing several nurses to come running. It was decided that she needed peace more than diversion. So off went the TV.

On the third morning, Rui received a police summons to answer questions and to remain at his home until the investigation was completed, which could take many months. Gwendolyn and Giles both knew that it would be the last time they would see him. She sniffled as tears rolled down her cheeks when Rui said his final farewell.

Giles was moved, too. He thanked Rui profusely for helping him find her. Without his plane and idea where George might be, they would never have found her. She could have sunk into madness, wandering aimlessly through the fields in her blood-soaked robe, eating scraps from trash cans. They hugged each other tightly then Rui left.

Giles was secretly glad that the victim of their crime was out of the picture. Gwendolyn was good about not calling him 'Giles', but she was not of completely sound mind. Who knows what she might have said to Rui without even knowing it? So, now it was just the two of them.

Another day passed before Gwendolyn finally stopped grieving that Rui had left. Giles tried to hold conversations with her, but she would go silent after a few minutes. He thought it might be a good idea to take her for a walk in the hospital garden. But when he opened the door of her room with her gripping his arm tightly, she cringed back with fear.

Giles was very much pained by how long it was taking for her to recover her bearings and be of right mind. Her doctor ordered a psychiatrist to spend some time with her. He had to leave when she came for her visits. He returned as the session was ending to inquire about her conclusions. She had none to share yet. She returned for two more days. By the end of the third session, she could do no more. It was up to Gwendolyn after that. After her final session with Gwendolyn, she met Giles in the hall outside her room.

"She has suffered extreme trauma. Will she recover? It's possible. But as with many others suffering from PTSD, it can come back at any time. Anything may trigger it. If she suffers from a PTSD attack, here is a prescription for her. You can fill it at the hospital pharmacy on the ground floor. Hopefully, with a few more days of peace and calm, she'll be ready to be released from the hospital. But then the hard work comes: helping her transition back into normal life.

"I strongly recommend taking her somewhere for a nice vacation where there is only peace and quiet. Do not take her on any flights or bus rides when she would be surrounded by strangers in a busy environment such as an airport or a bus station. Does she prefer mountains or the sea?"

"The sea," he responded.

"That's good because Portugal doesn't have many mountains worthy of the name. Fortunately, we have plenty of quiet and remote beaches. I would suggest looking at the southern coast of Alentejo. It's only a two to three-hour drive. If you don't mind spending some money, you could hire a private driver and car to take you both. If you go in the middle of the day in the middle of the week, you should have little traffic after crossing the bridge out of Lisboa.

"Hopefully, she'll recover completely, and she'll never have to use those pills. In my opinion, I think she will. She's young and has a strong personality. Please be patient with her. It might require more time than expected. Here's my phone number. Call me if there ever is an emergency.

"Another thing. Here is the phone number of Doctor Raquel Rocha. She has a private practice and specializes in PTSD trauma in hostage cases. She also worked for several years in the UN refugee camps for those brutalized by one of the never-ending civil wars in the Congo. I took the liberty of discussing Gwendolyn with her. She would gladly help when or if it's necessary. You clearly care very much for her. Good luck."

Giles thanked her and returned to the room. To his surprise, Gwendolyn was standing by the window and enjoying the grand vista of the sea.

"It's beautiful, isn't it?"

"Yes, dearest, it certainly is. How are you feeling?"

"I'm getting bored and, frankly, I need to get out of here. Let's leave tomorrow morning. Can you arrange that?"

"I'll check with the doctor. If he agrees, we'll do exactly that." He left and returned shortly.

"Great! He agrees! Your other doctor suggested we spend some time at a nice, quiet beachside resort on the southern Alentejo coast. I'll find one and organize a car and driver to take us there. Let's plan on leaving late in the morning. I'll need to go to the hotel first to check out and pick up our things before we go. Do you think you would be ready to leave at, say, 1030? If not, we can wait as long as you like."

"By the gods, no! I wish to be out of this place now. Hospitals make me nervous. Ocean waves calm me. That's where I need to be. But I refuse to go in nothing but this hospital gown. I seem to have lost my clothes; I mean the ones I was wearing before this. Maybe you could ask if the hospital could return them. I see my knapsack there in the corner. It doesn't have anything to wear either. It seems I hadn't packed for any longer than a day."

"The hospital doesn't have your clothes, dearest. I'm sure of it. Don't give it another thought. I'll bring the bags that you have left with me with all your clothes and other items. You can leave that gown behind. How about going for a stroll through the beautiful hospital garden?"

"Yeah, let's go. I feel like I need to be aired out. After that, I'll need to take a shower. My hair is in a complete mess."

The next morning at 1100, Giles checked Gwendolyn out of the hospital. Queirós made sure she was a guest of the generous people of Portugal and had taken care of all expenses. Then he led her carefully to a waiting van. The driver hopped out and opened the van's back sliding door.

Sitting on the back seat was a small cat carrier. Calico meowed when she saw Gwendolyn's joyful expression. She entered the van and took her fellow cult victim out of her cage. She held the precious little purring animal close to her. As she licked her face, peace and happiness filled Gwendolyn's heart. Calico did more for her than any doctor could.

Giles entered the van on the other side. Gwendolyn placed her hand on top of his. "Thank you, dear friend. Thank you for sticking by me. You saved my life. Without you, I would have been lost. And remembering Calico is just pure class."

"It would have been impossible for me not to. Let's go and enjoy some of this famous Portuguese sunshine by the sea. This is the time of year for fat, fresh grilled sardines. Driver! Let's go!"

EPILOGUE

The Emerald Sea Resort sat some twenty steps from the Atlantic, protected by cliffs to the northwest. The individual bungalows were one-bedroom suites with a full kitchen and a spacious living room. When all the sliding glass doors were opened, the wide veranda facing the ocean and the living room became a single space. The style of the interior decoration and furniture were different for each bungalow. Gwendolyn chose one in the manner of traditional Thailand.

The furniture was made of rattan and teak. The walls were adorned with painted rustic scenes of men and women doing various traditional agricultural activities, wearing nothing but colorful sarongs around their hips. Hand-woven rugs haphazardly covered the wooden plank floor. In the corner, a serene buddha sat in an ornate wooden shrine decorated with small multicolored bits of glass surrounded by wisps of incense. Fresh jasmine flowers completed the peaceful and sensual experience.

Giles chose the bungalow beside hers that happened to be in a vintage London style. It had the same layout as hers, but the similarity stopped there. Instead of teak and rattan, his furniture was made of dark cherry wood and leather. Cheerful vermilion red paisley wallpaper replaced the happy bucolic semi-nudes of Gwendolyn's. The floor to ceiling bookshelves held the classics on one wall and on another was a single massive mirror. Lighter-colored oak accented the rooms, and an old, red still-functioning British phone booth oddly occupied the same corner of the living room that held the meditating buddha in Gwendolyn's bungalow.

The bungalows were connected by winding paths of wood chips surrounded by spaces of grass liberally interspersed with colorful flower beds. Palm tree groves allowed for the interplay of light and shadow. All paths led to the large resort center. The roof was an A-frame two stories tall. The entrance was an entirely open space from the base to the apex of the A allowing the afternoon sun to completely fill the lobby and the reception area.

The resort had everything a convalescent could possibly need to find inner peace again, all contained in a beautiful, secluded corner of Alentejo. The restaurant ranged from Portuguese grilled fish to Indian curries, African stews to Asian stir-fried delicacies. An Olympic-sized swimming pool filled the need for serious exercise. The beach offered umbrella-covered divans for dozing to the steady rhythmic sound of waves. Comfortable massage tables were scattered around the beach, each accompanied by a calming masseuse prepared to give expert relaxation to tense bodies. A glass elevator took guests to the top of the cliffs rising behind the resort for hikes above the sea in a pine forest on trails blanketed with pine needles. The list could go on.

Gwendolyn smiled as she sat down on the broad teak sofa. The first thing she did was order a few unsalted grilled sardines for Calico and a mango lassi for herself. They had stopped at a pet store before arriving at the resort to get the things a cat requires such as treats and a cat box with litter. She set up Calico's cat box in a corner of the covered veranda. While unpacking, the sardines and lassi arrived. She and Calico enjoyed these on the veranda, facing the softly lapping waves of the ocean.

As the shadows lengthened, Gwendolyn laid in the large brass tub and took a warm bubble bath. A bottle of local Alentejo chilled white wine was within reach. After the bath water cooled to lukewarm, she put on a luxuriously thick bathrobe and made her way to the spacious canopy bed that filled her bedroom. She let the robe drop to the floor and stretched her limbs under the silk sheets. The soft smooth fabric moving across her nude body erased the tensions of the past few days. Before she fell asleep, Calico burrowed under the sheets and snuggled against the small of Gwendolyn's back.

Twenty hours later of deep dreamless sleep, she awoke to a furry purring pat to the nose. Hearing the birds chirping mingled with the sound of the sea, Gwendolyn felt peaceful, as if a great weight had been removed from her shoulders. She put on her bathrobe and gave Calico the leftover sardines. She stretched and yawned for a few moments before heading down to the beach where she ordered a full breakfast, though it was pushing on late afternoon. She finished with a two-hour massage to the melody of seagulls and waves.

After a long sleep, a satisfied stomach, and a relaxing massage, Gwendolyn felt ready to be sociable again. She decided to visit her next-door neighbor and caregiver whom she found sipping chilled sherry on his veranda. Incredibly, he had discovered in one of his bookcases the complete volumes of Edward Gibbon's The Decline and Fall of the Roman Empire.

"Oh, I see you have undertaken a project for the long haul. You'll need a barrel of sherry to accompany you on that voyage."

"She breathes! How are you?"

"Much better, thanks. I feel like I need the company of a friend for dinner tonight. Are you available?"

"Available? I'm here for you no matter how long it will take. As you can see, I've found a project that will amuse me. I haven't read this multi-volumed tome for at least twenty years. But the short answer is I would be honored. What time?"

"Eight?"

"Fine. I'll knock on your door at exactly eight. I think we're the only guests here. So, I doubt we need to make reservations."

"You can make them, anyway. I'll be expecting you to be on time. You shouldn't keep a lady waiting." With that, she smiled and left.

Even after a week of wonderful dinners, she was not very communicative. Giles was as charming as he could be, entertaining her with a wide range of absurd stories, some true and others imaginary. Gwendolyn smiled or laughed, but she was not in a talking mood. He remained patient, reading his The Decline and Fall of the Roman Empire, waiting for her to return to her normal self and the world.

Ten days after they checked in, she asked him if he would like to accompany her on a few hours' walk through the pine forest above the cliffs. He readily agreed. Soon after lunch, they ascended the elevator and found themselves at the edge of a deep forest, heavy with the scent of pine needles. The cool sea breeze rustled the branches above them, releasing the very pleasing pine fragrance.

Occasionally, the wind would knock off a pinecone from a high tree branch. It would drop to the needle covered forest floor with a muffled thump. They made a game of it. She would guess where it landed and retrieve   it. He carried them for her in his cloth sack that held their two water bottles.

They walked silently for a while. Gwendolyn pointed to a fallen log. Giles nodded in agreement, and they sat down. After watching the waves far below for some time, she broke the silence.

"Thank you so much for being with me, Giles. You really are a true friend. I'll never forget what you have done and continue to do for me."

"Oh, no need to thank me, dear girl. I have no choice but to take care of you, no matter what. What kind of uncle would I be to not look after his errant but very special niece?

She laughed and leaned her head on his shoulder. "Oh, yes, my dear 'Uncle' Giles. Where would I be without you?"

After a few moments, she sat up. "Look, I'm not sure what happened. I vaguely remember being in a moldy basement cell. I remember running through fields to escape, and in the end being returned to the cell after all my efforts. I was sitting on a hard rock bed with Calico on my lap. Before waking up in the hospital room, the last thing I remember is walking through the open cell door into complete darkness. It felt as if I stepped into a black hole that was the hellish gaping maw to a bottomless pit. I kept falling until I landed in my hospital bed.

"Wait. I seem to remember lying on another stone table with a demon standing above me with a knife ready to kill me. Then Calico jumped on my chest and saved me. Yes, I remember that, too. But it was all so outrageous, these strange nightmares. I don't know what to make of it all. Giles, what happened? How did I end up in the hospital?"

"You really don't remember anything for certain, do you? Maybe it's better that way."

"Oh, don't be like that! Tell me! What happened?"

"I wish I could tell you, Gwendolyn, but I wasn't there until the very end. I only know George was the one who kidnapped you."

"George! That devil in my dreams was George! Yes. Oh, by the gods, I'm starting to remember. But you're telling me that maybe it wasn't a dream? Really? Hm…" Her face turned from calm into a grimace.

She went silent. Giles was in way over his head. He did not want to say the wrong thing and make her trauma worse. "Look, I won't say anymore on this subject. This is way beyond me. Before we can even start to think about leaving here and going on to the next project, I need you to promise me something."

"Of course, Giles, what is it?" Her grimace relaxed to a frown.

"Gwendolyn, I consider you a very special and close friend. I want what is only best for you. You've been through way too much for one with the sensitive soul of an artist. If you want to quit now, I'd understand perfectly."

"What exactly are you saying? I love what I do and have no intention of quitting. I'm already bored here and want to get on with the next project. I know you have more than a few. So, which one should we start with?"

"You've endured some traumatic experiences. I was very worried about you in the hospital. I will not give you any new projects until I'm sure you're ready for them."

"Oh, now don't be like that. So, I fainted and spent some time in a hospital. I was kidnapped. You and the police rescued me. Yes, it was terrible, but nothing too terrible as you're making it out to be."

"Look, my dear, it was far worse than you realize. You've buried the memories. But the horrible experiences are still there. They'll appear to attack your peace of mind at any time in any place. They can happen at the wrong possible time. I can't allow that to happen."

"Giles! Don't make me plead. Don't make me beg!"

"Don't even think about getting on your knees. I'll tell you what. If you do just one thing for me, I'll consider it. But you must take this request extremely seriously, no matter how much time is required."

"I promise! I promise! What is it?"

"The hospital gave me a contact for a doctor who specializes in people who have suffered serious trauma like hostages and victims of war. I have already called her. Her name is Doctor Raquel Rocha. She has agreed to come and stay here to work with you every day, all day if necessary.

"If you take this seriously and work hard with her, you will be treated and cured. That, I'm certain. When she tells me you're ready, only then will we discuss the next projects. I don't care if it takes months or years. I'm not really interested in what you have to say about it either. I will only accept her professional decision. Do you agree?"

"Years? Giles, did you say years? But I feel fine. Yes, I have been having vividly terrible dreams lately. So, I don't sleep well. How's that serious?"

"Look, I'll not debate about it. Do you agree with my terms? If not, we'll have to part ways. I'll always hold you close in my heart like the daughter I never had. That'll never change. We would only be ending our professional relationship. Would you prefer that?"

"What? End our professional relationship? What are you saying, precisely?"

"I think you understand me perfectly well. Doctor Rocha can be here as early as tomorrow morning. This is about you, not me. She will be the difference between you living a full healthy life or being haunted by horrors that will only get worse until they affect your waking days as well. I don't mind staying here until she gives me the green light. I have arranged with the hotel that it will only be the three of us here. No expense is too much when it comes to you. What do you say? Do you agree or not?"

She silently stared at the waves crashing against the rocks at the foot of the cliff below for nearly ten minutes. Finally, she sighed and answered, "OK, I'll do it. My 'Uncle' Giles' advice has always been spot on. Why would it be any different this time?"

She smiled and gave her 'uncle' a big hug.

The End

FINAL THOUGHTS

Gwendolyn and Calico thank you very much for reading their story and they trust you enjoyed it. This is the result of many years of work. They ask you, dear reader, to please leave a thoughtful and considerate review on Amazon. These are especially important to the author. Please type it into your browser and you will be taken directly to the book page.
http://www.amazon.com/review/create-review?&asin=B0D64LM15C

ABOUT THE AUTHOR

Born in Philadelphia, Thomas Murray is foremost a storyteller and has been writing all his life. He is the author of The Eye of the Beholder, The Adventures of Nuno and Figo, Only After Dark, The Amazing Tale of Gwennie, and Ponce de León: A Modern Sequel. He currently lives in Portugal.

Having lived overseas for over twenty-five years on five continents and traveled to eighty-nine countries, he has trained his mind to be sensitive to the wide range of nuances and world views that make up the personalities of everyone he meets. Greatly appreciating global cultures, he includes many details about the places and characters to make readers feel they are part of the story. When he is not writing, he is travelling and learning foreign languages, currently Portuguese.

You can learn more about Thomas and his writing at
www.thomasmurraywriter.com

Please like his Facebook page: www.facebook.com/thmurraywriter

You can contact the writer at Bastet Publishing: info@bastet.ink

Also by the Same Author

The Eye of the Beholder, Bastet Publishing, 2020 (first in the Gwendolyn series)

A young art forger on the run …

Gwendolyn, a likable rogue with attitude, is secretly a successful fine-art forger rubbing shoulders with society's elite and shady art dealers. When she switches her painting with the original in a private home and escapes, she is confident with another successful heist. Until the next day when the owners are found murdered.

Framed for murder, she must travel to dangerous exotic lands to find the real murderers and clear her name. But as she delves deeper into the dangerous underworld of art forgery and betrayal, she realizes that she may be in over her head.

As the stakes get higher and her enemies close in, Gwendolyn must use all her cunning and skill to survive. Will she be able to untangle the web of lies and clear her name? Or will she become the next victim in a deadly game of cat and mouse?

https://www.amazon.es/dp/1735260606

The Adventures of Nuno and Figo: An Illustrated Journey of Two Unlikely Friends, Bastet Publishing, 2020 (first in the Gwennie series)

One clever rat, one tramp steamship, one hungry lynx …

Experience an adventure unlike any other. Follow Nuno, a clever Iberian Lynx, as he embarks on a treacherous journey to Southern California in search of a new life. Along the way, he meets Figo, a streetwise ship rat, who introduces him to the different cultures, music, and cuisines of the ports they visit.

Together, they face perils lurking around every corner as they form an unlikely friendship. Will it endure the journey, or will the dangers of California prove too difficult to survive? With beautiful illustrations by Madalena Bastos, this is a book you won't want to miss. The author will donate 10% of net proceeds to one or several organizations whose mission is to save the wonderful Iberian Lynx.

https://www.amazon.es/dp/1735260622

The Amazing Tale of Gwennie: Homeless to Palace, Bastet Publishing, 2022 (second and last in the Gwennie series)

From homeless cat to palace queen...

How did Gwennie journey from being a forlorn homeless cat in southern California to being the spoiled queen of a palace in Portugal? As the daughter of Nuno, an Iberian Lynx, and Terpsie, a Maine Coon cat, this (mostly) true story continues as the second in the series that started with The Adventures of Nuno and Figo: The Incredible Journey of Two Unlikely Friends (Illustrated). Gwennie travels to even more exotic places than her famous father. Follow her journey as she incredibly ends up in Portugal, the same country as her father's homeland, a half a world away.

https://www.amazon.es/dp/B0BCS7NNBX

Only After Dark: One Man's Descent into Obsession and Madness, Bastet Publishing, 2021

Prepare to be enthralled by a dark and beguiling world as an American author of horror discovers an alluring and mysterious existence beyond his own in the post-Revolution Portugal of the late 1970s. Running from his past, he moves into an abandoned crumbling palace, eager to make progress on his next bestselling novel. A chance encounter with an unnamed, yet shockingly sensual woman pulls aside the veil of the world to reveal an alluring existence defined by unnatural delights and mind-twisting hedonism.

As his mysterious lover draws him further into her realm of shadows and ultimate pleasure, how much is he willing to sacrifice to keep her? And will there be anything left of his sanity when his would-be goddess is through with him? A tale told in the vein of Lovecraft and Edgar Allen Poe, this book will have you on the edge of your seat and wanting more.

https://www.amazon.es/dp/1735260673

Ponce de León: A Modern Sequel, Bastet Publishing, 2022

What is the meaning of life if you can live forever?

What if 500 years ago Ponce de León did discover the Fountain of Youth? He and his crew have everything anyone could dream of: wealth, health, love of friends, and time; eternal time. But is immortality a blessing or a curse? Ponce de Léon is not so sure. He enters a personal crisis seeking this answer to the meaning of life. His search for answers leads him to a truth he never expected.

https://www.amazon.es/dp/173526069X

www.ingramcontent.com/pod-product-compliance
Lightning Source LLC
Chambersburg PA
CBHW020942180626
46814CB00003B/900